ONCE UPON AN EMPIRE

ONCE UPON AN EMPIRE

By Chuck Fleischmann

Made for Success Publishing
P.O. Box 1775 Issaquah, WA 98027
www.MadeForSuccess.com

Distributed by Blackstone Publishing

First Printing

Library of Congress Cataloging-in-Publication data
Fleischmann, Chuck
     Once Upon an Empire
          p. cm.

LCCN: 2024953102
ISBN: 979-8228310483

Printed in the United States of America

For further information, contact Made for Success Publishing
+1425-526-6480 or email service@madeforsuccess.net

I am thankful for so many people in my life: my parents, my wife, my children, my friends, and my everlasting well-wishers. However, I must dedicate this, my first novel, to Almighty God, who has bestowed upon me infinite blessings, especially the creativity to pen this work of political fiction.

Chapter 1

A Statesman Retires

The early December malaise had settled over Washington. Cold winter days dragged on in the waning hours of another Congress. The sullen gloom gripped the Capitol as members readied for the traditional holiday break. Christmas was nearing, and John Kinsley was less gloomy than usual. Two terms in the House, and he was going home—for good. As a forty-two-year-old lawyer, political science guru, and historian, he had grown tired of the "People's House." John never understood the Senate, pitied the Executive and Judiciary branches, and was finished with his personal endeavor in American Government optimism.

John finished packing up his congressional office for the final time. The benign eviction of him and his staff to make way for a newly-elected member arriving in January stung him a bit, but not for long. He reminisced for a while with a well-deserved pause. Four years earlier, he had arrived in the same recycled space, cluttered with the artifacts and apparatus from decades of predecessors. It was efficient, musty, and generic, yet tailored to fit its overall purpose.

Leaving his office, John smiled at his staff, who were also packing their things. He quipped, as he had hundreds of times before, "I'll make you proud," for one last time. The staff would soon be scattered over Washington like a newly shuffled deck for the House. They smiled back at John, and he walked away to the sound of muted chuckles.

John then began his walk from his office to the Capitol building. Although not a new walk, it was different this time, a parting hurrah at an early age. As he maneuvered up the steps, John looked across the gray day and smiled. The Capitol stood before him on the Hill. In its current condition, it had not changed since the Civil War. The dome adorned on two sides by the House and Senate steps was a constant reminder and fixture of D.C. Stepping inside, John murmured, "A monument to gridlock," then shook his head and navigated his way to the House Chamber.

The Floor was vibrant and happy, crowded with chairs and members speaking loudly in tens of separate conversations. As John stepped onto the Chamber's vibrant carpet, he looked up at the House gallery. Constituent onlookers peered down upon the active Chamber with interest reminiscent of zoo visitors.

Members chatted jovially, saying their goodbyes. For some, temporary; for others, permanent. They were technically gathered for the insignificant year-end suspension votes, closing out the waning hours of one Congress in preparation for a new Congress in January. So, at the station nearest his seat, John cast his final vote; the virtual wall at the front of the room lit up with a green "Y" next to his name. When his vote closed, the screen returned to its mundane but tasteful wallpaper until the next vote was called, sealing them in the annals of American history as ledger entries for the ages.

Out of the corner of his eye, John saw Chairman Jack making his way toward him. Chairman Jack was a congressional veteran with twenty-five years of service and counting. He was a creature of Washington and all it had to offer.

"John," Chairman Jack said in a solemn tone, "I'm sorry you have to go home so early. You had," he paused, "potential."

"I still do," John replied with a sigh. He didn't notice Jack's outstretched hand.

"I know you do," Jack said, "but I meant here. I love this place, John, this House, this city."

John leaned back, grinning widely. "Yes, you do. This is your world."

Perceiving the slightest of slights in John's reply, Jack responded, "Then, what's wrong with this place? This town is designed for us: pay your dues, scratch the right backs, play the game, and inevitably, you'll win." Jack chuckled and pushed his point further, "Heck, even if you are a loser here, you can still win. Nowhere else in America is like that."

John shook his colleague's hand, finally realizing it was outstretched. "It's just not for me, Chairman, just not for me."

They smiled at each other, convinced of their own positions, and simultaneously said, "Wish you the best."

John meandered the aisles across the House floor for a few final handshakes, hugs, and smiles. He exhaled and sighed; he was at peace.

John was pensive that morning and sad because the world Chairman Jack loved so much could and would continue; however, he'd come to peace with this, knowing he could not change the status quo in four years or, in his view, ever.

Four years earlier, a bright, successful attorney had come to Washington with a conservative but populist resolve, teeming with optimism. After two terms of self-inflicted agony, it seemed an eternity to John: speeches, meetings, fundraisers, words on words buoyed by the dreams of a political scientist turned lawyer. John had prided himself in his educational past: a grandiose thinker turned constitutional lawyer and, finally, a determined public servant. John believed he had been trained to figure out the Washington game. But, in fact, the game had worn him out, beaten his ideals badly without as much as a scratch upon the surface of the D.C. diamond.

John walked to the front of the Chamber for one last look and leaned against the Speaker's dais, pondering his next move. He had been so busy wrapping up his term that he suddenly realized he had given no thought to what he would do next. Return to the practice of law? Teach or lecture? All he could think of was being out of D.C.

John, though disappointed he had not changed Washington, was not bitter. He was resigned to his failure to change the world he was about to leave. The power structure, replete with lobbyists, bureaucrats, and D.C. insiders, was still intact, stronger than ever, but at least he found solace in one minor triumph: no more fundraising. It was with this comfort that he turned away from the Chamber for the last time.

As he walked off the Floor and through the less-than-hallowed halls of the Capitol building, John looked up and saw old Sam Grudger. Grudger was a lobbyist's lobbyist, traditional in both scope and trade: pay dues, honor authority, make friends, and lead with money. Grudger's wrinkles bore the scars of a thousand fights over tidbits and treasure in the federal domain. He was worn from the effects of age, savvy from the plunders of countless campaigns, and jaded by the accepted norms of a world of blurred lines. Grudger smiled at John and began, "Almost done, John."

John sheepishly smiled at the rugged lobbyist. He had always liked Grudger, even though he represented everything

John had come to loathe about Washington. Grudger, grinning with a defining squint in his left eye, robustly embraced John and implored, "John, come work for me."

John, now less timid in his parting refusal, just smiled back and said, "No, Sam. No." Feeling more confident, John grasped the aged lobbyist by the shoulders and, without pause, bore his homage aloud, "Ever since I arrived here, you have been like an uncle to me." Sam listened carefully to the young idealist as he continued, "Even when I opposed you, you were always willing to help and be a mentor. Thanks."

The older man merely grinned.

"Sam, you are 'old school.' I like that, always did. I, too, am built that way."

Grudger, always a beacon of praise, beamed through his wrinkled façade. "John, I always liked you, too. I don't understand you, though. Supposed to hate what I do and what I stand for, yet you like me." Now filled with a dose of praise, the old man continued, "I represent this town and all that it is. Despite your rhetoric and votes, I've always believed that part of you craved what I stand for, what I win for."

John listened intently, hanging onto every word of the aged icon.

"Yes, John," Sam continued, "I think I give you an odd sense of security, a foe you love to hate, but deep down, you love my game and respect it." Sam rested and waited for a response.

John grinned to remove any hint of an adversarial tone and replied, "No, Sam, but thanks. You may be right, but I've written, spoken, dreamed, and opined what I want government to be." He stammered briefly, correcting himself, "What I *wanted* it to be. And this is not it."

John paused to think for a moment, wondering if he should share his thoughts and finally decided to give it a shot. "Sam, perhaps I should write. Maybe a grand political treatise: the freedom to think outside of a set realm or world. The ability to wish, in this place or any other place, under the control of humankind."

Grudger, with his one eye squinted and the other wide open, stared at the parting legislator. "I knew you would reject my job offer, but it was sincere," he finally said.

John laughed briefly. "I didn't doubt it."

Grudger continued, "John, in another place or time, we could have been partners."

Now emboldened by the course of the conversation, John stuck out his hand, stared into Grudger's ruffled face, and said, "I'll settle for friends." They shook hands, and John began to walk away.

With a low, urgent interjection, Grudger stopped John in his tracks. "John, I have a proposal."

John turned back, forced out a laugh, and quipped, "Not another job offer, Sam."

"No, not another job offer, or at least, not one in the sense you are thinking."

John immediately recognized the Beltway double talk, which had become his all too frequent vernacular. Sam grew instantly serious and stern. He re-approached John with an intense gaze. "I knew an aspiring politician once who wrote a paper, something about an ideal state?"

John froze and whispered, "You read my paper?"

Sam nodded. *The Principles of the Ideal State* by John A. Kinley."

"Wow, I'm impressed. Really, I am. No one has read me in years, or at least, no one has mentioned that to me in a long time. Wow!" John paused, shaken by this revelation. Many years ago, he'd published a political treatise in the classical sense, not unlike the ancient philosophers who wrote and opined about the creation, maintenance, and existence of the ideal state. John's work laid out a blueprint for a new nation created from nothing into a working, living entity. "It was an obscure work, seldom read. I thought it was forgotten by the ages."

Grudger, fully aware he had John's undivided interest and attention, continued with his stern demeanor and pressed John, "I represent a group of, well, let's just say 'investors.' Philanthropists of sorts, and I have a proposal." Pausing, Grudger motioned to a thick ledge of a nearby Capital window. "Come, let's sit briefly and chat," Grudger offered.

Curious, John followed.

The sun shone through the Capitol window, highlighting Grudger's straggled hair and coal-gray eyes as he plied his trade upon his inquisitive interlocutor. "John, I have represented just about every issue and interest in this town in my time. Made millions." He paused and grinned. "No, billions with the anonymous tips I received."

John glanced around the empty hall, watching for passersby before his attention returned to the older man.

"I learned early on not to ask why or who. I'd just take it, run with it, and win . . . most of the time, of course. But this deal, John," he continued quietly, "is the biggest deal I've ever done. I promise it's huge—*earth-shattering*."

John was more interested than ever. "Why are you telling me this, of all people? I'm done. I'm out of this world, out of this city, devoid of a pin or voting card—a literal powerless walking ghost among the pillars of D.C." John pressed on, "You know this place. It rewards the politically living and ignores the politically dead."

Without missing a breath, Sam answered, "John, you are right! That is exactly why my clients want you. You are different, John, a visionary. They have followed you closely. Meet me at my office tomorrow; no obligation other than the truth. Just listen to them."

John nodded to the elder non-statesman with a tepid assent. Grudger winked at John with his one good eye, and they parted.

Chapter 2

The Proposal

John awoke the next morning at six and showered. He quickly combed his light brown hair into his usual neat style and then dressed in his favorite navy suit. Instinctively, he reached for his lapel pin. At the start of a new term, all of the members of the House receive the same pin in the spirit of unity. The pin is to be worn at all times in the Chamber. This was the second pin that John had received; it was a symbol of his former rank. Instead of fastening it to his lapel like he had every morning for the last four years, he laid it on his night table with his now obsolete voting card, tightened his favorite red, white, and blue tie, and departed for Grudger's office. He decided to walk the short distance to Grudger's law firm in downtown D.C., as he had done several times before. Upon arrival, he was greeted in the front office by Nan, the office manager.

The petite woman looked up at him sweetly. "Congressman Kinley, good morning."

John politely replied, "Just 'John' today, Nan."

Nan smiled broadly, crinkling the skin around her bright blue eyes. "You remembered my name. Thank you."

"No, thank you."

Still smiling, Nan said, "I'll take you back now."

John entered the firm's conference room. It was immaculate with a sterile, cold sense of sobriety. He'd been there many times before, but the discussions were always the same: asking for help with an issue, a vote, a cause, or a project. Those meetings and memories were all blurred now. Grudger stood and greeted John. He was dressed in his lobbyist's finest, adorned with gold accessories.

"Welcome to the Grudger Firm," he boomed as if this was John's first visit.

"Where the truth always matters, but the results always count!" John quipped. "I value the truth more than anything, Sam, and here, the results run rampant."

Sam nodded in dismissal, his left eye squinting tighter than usual in his excitement, and moved quickly to the topic at hand. "John, meet my clients," Sam hesitated and then corrected himself, "I mean, my associates, that is."

Three well-groomed men sat at the conference table and stared at John with a trio of neutral expressions. Somewhere in their sixties, they were strikingly alike, with pale blue eyes, trimmed gray hair, and pale coloring. All three were dressed immaculately in fine suits with matching thin blue ties. Their silent stares made John's skin crawl.

After several long, silent moments with no volunteered introduction, Grudger cleared his throat. He looked at John and exclaimed, "This is Mr. Combs, Mr. Burns, and Mr. Amos. They call themselves the CBA," he explained, "and they represent a very specific group of investors."

The three suited men stood, shook John's hand, and sat down with no show of emotion whatsoever. John was a bit taken aback by their conduct, especially in contrast to Grudger's flagrant behavior. He decided to be quiet as well and feign stoicism.

Combs silently motioned with his hand toward Grudger as if to command a servant to serve. Grudger, quick to obey, began, "John, I'll get right to the point; these men have studied you: your career, your writings, the whole Kinley package. I won't say they like or admire you, or anything or anyone for that matter." The three CBA men looked up at once, still silent but a bit ruffled by Grudger's last remarks. Grudger, seemingly trying to appease all present parties, leaned across the table, looked directly at John, and blurted out their proposal. "How would you like to be the founder of a state?"

Puzzled by this offer, John remained silent. Unfazed, Grudger continued, "I mean, a nation-state, a country. It would be all yours to do right by from the start." John looked at the three partners, waiting for some emotion or a smile, but there was nothing—just quiet stares. Undaunted, Grudger continued, "John, you could build your country—your vision, you might say—one nation under John."

That characterization struck a chord in John's ego, and his bewilderment turned to inquiry. He turned from Grudger and looked once again at the three men carefully studying him.

"Why me?" he asked them. "What's the catch? I have more questions for you."

Grudger said, "Ask away, John, but for now, only I will answer."

Combs, Burns, and Amos just nodded in quiet assent, their eyes fixed upon John in cold assessment.

Still skeptical of the entire conversation, John sarcastically shook his head with a forced smile, pointed at the silent men with a wandering arm, and quipped aloud, "Are these investors just going to give me a country? D.C. made me a skeptic, but really, my own country?"

Sam leaned forward, his good eye wide open, and smiled broader than John had ever seen. He nodded and said, "John, come take a trip with us. The land was purchased in South America, the funds are all set aside, and the boundaries are marked. The consortium is ready to begin next week."

John stood up abruptly, dazed by this strange offer, and blurted out a "But—"

He was forcefully interrupted by Grudger, "John, the *why* is not for me to discuss now."

The CBA trio was still silent, almost directing Grudger with their leers, stares, and loaded eye contact. John was not satisfied by the answers or demeanors on display, so he turned to Grudger. "What's in it for you?" he demanded.

Grudger grimaced at John's uneasy tone and demand but composed himself in front of the CBA. He looked up and smiled at John. "A big payoff, the biggest yet."

The CBA trio stared wantonly at the two men without comment. Grudger continued, "And then I'm done. I'm done. It's yours and theirs." Grudger was moving about the room in a sordid, swaying manner. "You can even bar my kind from your new world, John." This caused Grudger to laugh aloud, the first sincere bout of laughter he'd had since the meeting had begun. "Build your team, your vision."

Reeling from the magnitude of the prospect, John looked between the emotionless entourage and Grudger and said, "Thank you, I think." He paused. "I must reflect on all that's been said here today. You've given me a lot to think about, and it sounds too good to be true. I try not to be skeptical, despite the influence of my former profession, but it is a lot, even for my optimism."

Grudger jumped in, "Your optimism is why they want you, John. It's why *we* want you."

John felt obligated to continue, especially in light of the magnitude of what seemed to him unfathomable. He looked to the CBA trio and calmly said, "This whole idea is beyond me. Surely, you gentlemen don't jest. You're serious, very serious. But this meeting has been staggering for me. Surely, you must understand that." The CBA remained silent. John, though intrigued, was still uneasy. He implored them, "Please, be honest with me. I value the truth more than anything."

Realizing his oratory was still falling upon deaf ears and emotionless eyes, John decided to press on further. "How long do I have to decide?" he asked the four would-be bestowers of sovereignty.

Grudger looked at his watch and tersely replied, "One week from today, or the opportunity passes to another." He was clearly displeased that John had not immediately accepted his offer.

Combs, Burns, and Amos stood up simultaneously, nodded at Grudger and John, and walked out—no further handshakes, niceties, or pleasant goodbyes. It was an emotionless exit to an exciting meeting, at least for John. He and Grudger were left alone in the room, both drained in light of the past discourse. They sat silently for minutes, pondering their next moves.

Sam, known for his love of a good, stiff drink, broke the silence. "Want a drink?"

Still bewildered by the events at hand, John, a temperate idealist, answered, "No need to start now. In light of what you just offered, I need every tool of reason available to me, and sobriety has always been an asset. Have one for me, though."

Pouring his favorite bourbon, Sam smiled. "I will," he said as he quaffed a morning aperitif. Still in salesman mode, he persisted. "Let me continue."

"No, no," John interrupted. "Listen to me. I've always liked you and admired you too, but from afar. You represent a world I vowed to change and couldn't. You've succeeded in cause after cause, seemingly without pause or passion, almost robotically. That's not me." He paused, gulping a deep breath. "I wish I knew what was up with this whole thing. Why me? Why now? And how? Sam, darn it, what's the truth in all of this?"

Grudger, still nursing the remnants of his Kentucky favorite, just lifted his glass and said, "The truth is what you make it, whatever you want it to be."

John replied, "That's your world, not mine. Truth is not some relative concept to observe from afar; it's real, grounded, and, of course, true."

Sam, unfazed by the idealist's spouting, lifted his glass, tilted it toward John, and took his final sip. Then he declared again, "Truth shall be truth, but I need an answer in one week."

John sighed aloud and looked down sullenly as if he had been beaten in a debate. Without another word, he shook Sam's hand and left the conference room.

As John passed Nan on his way out of the office, she eyed him. "Good meeting, John?" she asked.

"I think so," he said tepidly. He was exhausted, drained, and left wondering what had just transpired.

"Good, good. Be well, sir," she said politely.

John murmured his thanks and departed, still stunned by the meeting. This was not the start of the new post-Congress life he had envisioned. Subdued, John walked back to his apartment, wondering what had just happened to him. He searched for an emotion—something to give name to everything happening inside of him. Finally, he settled on awe, simply awe.

CHAPTER 3

The Decision

John went about the rest of the day numb and emotionally detached. Going through the motions, he attended lunch at the DC Club, saying a few more somber goodbyes to friends and staff. In the evening, he boarded a flight back home to Indiana.

Upon landing, he tentatively reached for his phone to call Carlene LeFaze. John had been unduly fond of Carlene for years. In her presence, the sure-tongued, handsome lawyer was often inept, inarticulate, and clumsy. Only in her presence did this self-confident, steady statesman feel uneasy, awkward, and timid. John had long ago conceded to his inner self that he was smitten with Carlene and had to live with that affliction.

John gently touched his direct dial and waited for an answer on the other end—three, four rings. The call connected, and before Carlene was even able to say hello, he began, "Carlene, hi, it's John. How about an early dinner at the Indy Club?"

Carlene readily accepted. "Sure. The Club at six?"

"Yes, of course. Only the best for you—the Indy Club, our club. See you there." John realized that he was bumbling and talking too fast. He made himself relax. Despite the nerves, he was looking forward to their rendezvous.

John drove home to his Indiana abode, dressed instinctively in his holiday best with only Carlene on his mind. He dropped his things off hastily, not bothering to unpack, and then hit the road again. Driving to the Indy Club, John reminisced about his life as a young single lawyer and his first encounter with Carlene.

As an aspiring lawyer in his twenties, he'd attended a Bar association party in Indiana where he'd eyed Carlene from across the festive room. She was radiant and impeccably dressed with beautiful dark brown hair. He moved closer, catching a glimpse of her piercing brown eyes. And her presence—it was indescribable. He stared at her, stunned and silent, as he felt a trance-like grip take hold of him. Awe struck, dumbstruck, beauty struck, he knew not. He was immobilized with glee and completely infatuated with her.

John, the confident young lawyer, the widely popular talk of the town, approached Carlene and introduced himself with hesitation. "H-hi," he stammered, "I'm John."

Carlene looked at him with firm resolve. "Carlene." She immediately sensed his uneasy demeanor, chuckled, and relished it. "You okay?"

"Oh, yes," John replied. "Fine. It's just, well, it's been a busy day." Realizing his unartful groping for words, he inquired, "What do you do?" As he spoke with her, he was drawn to her beauty and focused on her every move.

"I'm the office manager at Crisp. You know Crisp, the best law firm in town?"

John, who was hanging onto every word and ignoring her boastful confidence, reached out for agreement. "Sure, I do," he said, "Crisp, fine firm."

She did not relent. "No, the *best*, not just fine."

Wanting to gain favor in any way possible, John just smiled at her with an infantile gaze. Unaware of her contrived banter, he eagerly hoped to gain her attention.

"So, what do you do?" she wryly inquired.

Carlene was feigning ignorance. She knew John was a successful lawyer, had made his first million in the practice, and was the rising star of the Bar. John, a quasi-celebrity in Indianapolis due to his success, opulence, and media savvy, was almost a household name. But she would not concede anything in their chat, and he was glad to accommodate her inquiry.

"I'm a lawyer," he said plainly without flash or swagger.

Carlene grinned, enjoying the surprising control she felt over her new acquaintance, and quipped, "Really, a lawyer at a Bar association party? Well done, John, well done."

Totally missing her controlled sarcasm, he pleaded his case, stammering a bit, "I mean, I'm a good lawyer, successful."

Sensing his uneasy delivery but dogged insistence, she queried, "Are you?"

He replied, "Yes, successful and articulate."

She moved closer to him, looked at him with a broad smile, and tauntingly replied, "I can see that." John was at a loss for words but still elated that she was conversing with him at all. Carlene had complete control of the dialogue, and she knew it. Still looking at him, she asked, "Married?"

"No, not yet," he said, "but someday, I mean, someday, yes, I hope. You?"

"Once," she said abruptly. "A failure. Him, I mean." She laughed dryly as she caught herself in a burst of irksome reflection. "Just never got there," she said.

John nodded understandingly. "I see." Sensing that he had monopolized her time, he hesitantly stuck out his hand, "So, good to know you."

She shook his hand firmly. "Know me, John? I think not, but still, nice to meet you." She scored another point in their discourse, having won every point so far.

Discombobulated by this stunning new acquaintance, in a parting inquiry, John managed to say, "Coffee?"

After a pause, she replied tauntingly, "Coffee what?"

"I mean, coffee sometime. You and me?"

"I guess." She winked at him again. He smiled broadly for the first time in their discussion.

Just as they were about to separate, Judge Smith came up to both of them. Smith was the senior Circuit Court Judge. Old money, gracefully reeking of affluence, and a cherished antique of the establishment in Indiana. "Carlene," he said, "I see you've met the finest young lawyer in our city, maybe our state."

John smiled with relief at the judge's comments. Carlene, smiling but not conceding a compliment to her new-found admirer, merely smiled and said, "Your Honor, it's so good to see you."

John was thankful for a vote of confidence after his posturing for Carlene. He said, "Thank you, Judge. It's good to see you." They shook hands, smiled, and separated.

Carlene was momentarily bothered by the change of momentum of their chat, so in a parting comment, she ribbed John one last time, "Coffee soon?"

"Oh, sure," he said, "Coffee soon, for sure."

A decade later, John remembered every word of that first meeting as if it had just happened. Coming out of memories of the past, John pulled into the Indy Club's parking lot. The building's brick facade was adorned for Christmas with unique elegance. Faint classical music soothed his rising nerves as he walked through the front door. He was met by a familiar face; Louie had been a fixture at the Club for years.

"Congressman," Louie boomed, "Merry Christmas!"

Shaking his hand, John smiled. "Not 'Congressman' anymore, Louie. Just glad to be home."

Louie grinned at John and just said, "She's already here, John, at your table, of course."

"Thanks. Merry Christmas."

John ambled through the club, taking in the familiar old-money décor, just as neat and orderly as he'd remembered it. Carlene was seated at "their table" in the back. He approached her. She was still radiant and perfectly dressed. He'd known her a decade, but he instinctively hesitated before stepping forward to hug her gently.

"Hi," he said meekly.

She smiled and replied, "Always good to see you, John. I remembered our table."

That brought a pleased smile to John's face. He sat down, and they dined on roast meats and other delicacies, their meal accented by the aroma of the club's two old-fashioned bars.

About five minutes in, Carlene asked eagerly, "What's next? I'm sure a young, retired congressman of forty-two has a lot of offers."

John could not help but boast about his accomplishments when it came to Carlene. He was powerless to his need to impress her. "Oh," he said, "so many offers. I'll have to sit and think there are so many." He sat looking at her as he had for a decade, fixated on her striking beauty, totally engulfed in all she was. "Hey, it's almost New Year's!" he exclaimed.

"Worry about Christmas first, John," she teased, evading the subject of the New Year.

For John, it sparked a memory of New Year's Eve almost a decade ago. They'd made a mutual promise to toast each other at midnight wherever they might be, together or apart. They were apart that year, but John wrote a poem about her, *Ode to the Radiance of Love*. John had always been a prolific writer, but this was his best work to date. When he saw her in January, his poem in hand and ready to read, she told him regrettably that she'd forgotten to toast him. She was busy with others or some flippant excuse. John was crushed. He never felt the same way about New Year's Eve again. Her "oh well" excuse left him hoping for a redo, which sadly never came. He stored the poem in his safe at home, hoping to read it to her someday.

They continued their meal, and with each passing minute, John felt more enamored with Carlene. They chatted about law, Congress, and, of course, Carlene.

"Dating?" he inquired.

"Not really," she replied.

Then, John asked timidly, "Miss me?"

She laughed. "Of course. Who wouldn't miss John Kinley, author, lawyer, statesman, and my suitor, not necessarily in that order or importance."

He perked up at that retort. She had controlled him again with relative ease and minimal effort. She continued, "So what are you going to do? I'm interested. Conquer the world, I hope?"

John was tentative. "Maybe," he said. He reflected for a moment on his career and on what he would do next. Filled with melancholy nostalgia, he blurted out, "I was good, you know?"

Carlene responded, "Yes, you were." She looked at him with the kindest look she seemed to be able to muster.

He replied, "But never good enough for you."

"That's not fair, John," she replied.

"I understand. It's just, well, I still suffer from Abe Quinn syndrome." She sat motionless while he pined.

Both were acutely aware of the situation he was referring to. Two years before he ran for Congress, John, the flashy litigator, had run to the scene of an accident where a reckless driver struck the rear of Carlene's car. John spent every day for a week calling on her, checking on the mild effects of whiplash, and trying to convince her to hire him for free so he could care for her in the best way he knew how. She took his visit, flowers, and calls, and then, without notice, she hired her then-lover's lawyer, Abe Quinn, for the case. Quinn, on his best day, could barely find the courthouse. He was a lovely man, though, and ran unpaid tabs for hapless clients for years. When Quinn called John to tell him the news, John slumped to the floor, his chest aching from the pain of her rejection. He had been so sure Carlene would accept his offer of assistance. John was devastated for days.

Finally, he ran into Carlene on the street about two weeks later. Without a reason or care, she trivialized the situation, oblivious to his feelings, and merely said, "Surely Quinn can handle that little legal matter."

John could not understand how she could hurt him without any compunction whatsoever. That was just Carlene.

Years later, on the eve of closing his law practice on the way to Congress, John confided in Carlene that he loved her but had never gotten over her rejection in the car wreck case. He gazed into her cold eyes and tried to explain to her that he never regained his confidence as a lawyer after she rejected his offer of legal help. There were no apologies that night and no explanations. Today was no different. Carlene didn't deign to reply to his comment. As they left the club together, he hugged her and asked, "When?"

She considered him. "Call me when you decide what you are going to do."

On his drive back home that evening, after a long, strong dose of Carlene, John was content. Her questions on what he would do next stirred his thoughts, turning him once again toward Grudger's offer. Was this a hoax? A joke? What exactly was the reason for such a proposal? He was still pondering, still baffled by it all. As he drove home, he passed Saint Jude, his home church, and decided to stop. He entered, knelt in the empty pews, and prayed for guidance and strength. Even so, John left the church an hour later, just as lost. That night, John didn't sleep at all. He tossed and turned, thinking of first the CBA deal and then Carlene. John bounced between agitation and confusion. When he arose, he finally landed on a decision and called Grudger.

"Sam," he said. "Let's take a trip."

Chapter 4

The Flight

John arrived at the airport tarmac to find a huge unmarked jet. A stern but pleasant attendant greeted him at the base of the boarding stairs. "Mr. Kinley?" she asked, a smile breaking underneath her red lipstick.

He nodded.

"Please come with me."

Following the attendant up the stairs, John boarded the plane to find only Grudger on board, drink in hand and grinning. "Come in, John. This is all for you!"

Confused, John asked, "Where are the three wise men?"

"They've been where we are going. It's just us for now, my friend."

John was full of questions. "How long is the flight?"

Sam lounged, sipping his drink. "Relax, John, it's hours. Ten or so, I think." This did not narrow down the list of potential destinations nor eliminate John's questions, but as Sam was clearly not feeling forthcoming, John did as he said and relaxed into one of the comfy seats on the jet. He had to admit that the CBA plane was by far the largest, most luxurious plane he'd ever been on.

The flight was uneventful. John and Sam spoke of things unrelated to the offer at hand. They swapped stories of old D.C. and Sam's youth. John felt surprisingly at ease, but after several hours, John returned to his questioning. "When do we land?"

"We don't land," Grudger said carefully. "Not yet."

His answer made John ill at ease. He murmured, "Okay then."

Shortly thereafter, Grudger led John to the cockpit. The pilot and co-pilot were friendly, welcoming the two passengers to their space. Through the front window, the open sky was bright and clear. The view from the cockpit was breathtaking. As far as their eyes could see, lush forests were untouched by the hand of mankind and beaming with the glow of radiant shades of green. The virgin landscape was alluring, with a strong sense of potential.

Suddenly, after a nod from the pilot, Grudger told John, "Look down there, John."

John leaned forward and observed. "It's land, just miles and miles of land."

"Exactly, open land for miles and miles." Grudger's smile widened.

Puzzled, John asked, "What's so exciting about open land? By the way, where are we?"

Grudger looked him right in the eyes. "We're somewhere around north-central South America. And this land below? We bought a plot of it about the size of Delaware, maybe a bit larger. And now it's all yours."

Shocked and intrigued by the revelation, John inquired further, "How did we get the land?"

"A purchase from three or so South American countries. It's done. No worries. All the details have been signed, sealed, and delivered by our CBA friends."

John listened intently. In a state of subdued elation, Sam continued, "There's plenty of forest, plains, some mountains; it's beautiful. This can be yours for the taking—excuse me," he paused with a sneaking smile, "making."

The plane abruptly turned, the pilot explaining, "Going to Chile to refuel."

"Then, we'll head home," Grudger told John.

For the rest of the plane ride, John barraged Grudger with questions. The picture Grudger and the CBA painted was alluring but almost unbelievable. Grudger seemed to feel confident that he had tipped the scales of this deal in his favor, so he encouraged John to ask away.

"Okay, Sam, let's see. You want me to use this land to build a nation, just like that?"

"Yes," Sam replied, reclining in his spacious leather seat.

"But what's the catch? Why me? Why now?"

Without hesitation, Grudger answered, "Why does it matter? It's yours, all yours."

"Mine for what reason, Sam? Surely, there's more to this. An ask, a catch, constraints, what?"

"No, no," Grudger insisted. "No hidden clauses or constraints." Leaning in, he pressed, "Just say yes." Grudger, not one known for a quiet approach, then whispered to John, "There's a trillion dollars in reserve for you in a central bank at your beck and call. Build a state, a nation, exactly the way you want it."

"But," John persisted, "Those three men, the CBA, who are they? Who do they represent? There are too many unanswered questions."

Undaunted, Grudger replied, "John, they chose you. I chose you, John Kinley, the eternal optimist. You left a town of skeptics, cynics, and naysayers because you couldn't change it. Just say yes, and all of that is behind you. You become the artist, the creator. Don't worry about the details; you'll make the details. Don't worry about the rules; you'll make the rules. Think of it: a new nation built from scratch, start to finish. Land, money, laws, it's all up to you. You decide, and we provide."

John sat back in his seat and thought deeply. What if he said yes? What would he build, and how would he build it? Where would he start? He thought of his writings. *The Principles of the Ideal State* included blueprints for governing by truth, incorruptible leadership at all levels, economic freedom, and a steadfast commitment to the conservative values gleaned from and preserved by Western civilization. Those ideals still inspired him. The subtle mix of intoxicating power, control, and especially the vision of his own country had John craving a way to say yes.

John came out of his tumultuous trance with another question for Grudger. "So, what's in it for you?"

Grudger laughed and said, "All right, John, I'll tell you straight up. You say yes, and I'll make a lot of money and go away. You say no, I'll make no money and still go away. It's just that simple. As a matter of fact," Sam continued, "You can outlaw my kind in your new utopia."

John looked at Grudger, smiled, and said, "I might need more of your kind if I say yes."

They both laughed.

John knew Sam wanted an answer. A big payoff awaited an affirmative response. Sometime between taking off from Chile and landing in Indiana, John had settled on a yes. He did not convey this to Grudger; however, he was hoping to extract more information from the lobbyist about his client and the deal. He merely informed Sam that he would let him know the next day, feeling a growing sense of confidence and power. The plane landed, and John and Sam parted as if returning from a regular business trip.

John looked at Grudger before departing. "Thanks, Sam. I'll let you know tomorrow."

Grudger smiled back with a final response, "I got you, John. I got you."

The older man knew John was hooked.

CHAPTER 5

The Set Up

After leaving the airport, John was zipping along the drive toward home when he realized his new country would have no roads. In fact, it would have no cars. In reality, it would have nothing at all. Nothing but money, land, and promise. He realized he was under no confidentiality agreement, but whom would he tell of this bizarre yet wonderful news? Who would believe him or, more importantly, believe *in* him? His thoughts went immediately to Carlene, always Carlene. Surely, she would be thrilled that he had been chosen for such a project. He dialed her from the car.

"Hey, got a minute?"

"Sure. Miss me that much already?" she teased.

The new founder, who had been boosted in confidence several fold by the CBA offer, had a momentary lapse in hubris and responded with a fluttering, "Kinda."

"Kinda," she said, "that's not flattering, John."

John was solely focused on his newfound opportunity. With a strong, logical tone, he made his pitch. "How would you like to found a nation with me? A country, a new land?"

"John," Carlene said. "You don't drink, never do drugs, and I realize I have staggering effects on you, but wow, John, you sound nuts, really nuts. You've lost it this time. I pity you."

"Listen, Carlene, it's true. I'll have land, money, power, and whatever I need to build whatever I wish." He continued, "You could be the First Lady of a one-of-a-kind endeavor."

He was met with silence on the other end of the phone, so he pleaded further, "When I was a lawyer, I was never good enough for you. Not as your lover or your lawyer, never good enough. Surely this could do it for you? You would be an empress for the ages, Carlene." He eagerly awaited an answer, which was forthcoming and harsh.

"John," Carlene insisted, "You never were my lawyer." He winced. "As for love, oh, well, you tried. But this, this is nuts. Grow up," she crowed. "Someone has fooled you, tricked you. Be a lobbyist or consultant. Do something consequential and then call me! Until then, we're just, for lack of a better term, friends."

John was crushed by her harsh barbs, which reopened wounds that had never fully healed. Each word stung him with relentless pain. Achingly, he felt compelled to respond like a lightweight, beaten badly and pushed to swing one last time before falling to the canvas. He managed to say, "Friends? No friend would ever leave me in the condition you have time and time again. This deal is real, not a once-in-a-lifetime, but a once-in-an-eternity. It will be our empire, our love, our chance, at last."

Carlene was unmoved, "It's fiction. I wish you well and leave you to the ages." She hung up without waiting for him to reply.

John sped the rest of the way home, frustrated with Carlene while still intoxicated by the CBA offer. He pulled into his driveway and dialed Grudger.

"I'll do it. I'm in." John was livid, and it showed.

Grudger responded, "Fine, but I thought you would be happier about it. You seem annoyed."

John realized he almost sounded ungrateful, but he was still reeling from Carlene's effects. In his disappointment, he merely replied, "I just thought I'd have a partner along for the ride."

Knowingly, Sam said, "Now that we have a deal, here's some free advice—and in my line of work, nothing is free. Who is that petite brunette friend of yours?"

"Who?" John replied. "Carlene?" John and Sam had discussed personal matters briefly over the past four years of working in close proximity to each other, so it wasn't surprising that Sam had a basic understanding of John's connections, but he had never offered an opinion before.

"No, no," Grudger said. "She's awful. I mean the teacher: sweet girl, attentive, and oh so kind. She's the right choice for your partner."

John reflected, then spoke, "Mary? Why Mary?" John had known Mary since childhood. The two of them had dated on and off for years, and the off was always on him. John, ever ambitious, always wanted more of a challenge. Fortunately for him, Mary was a committed teacher, always wanting her children to succeed, and she was practiced at being flexible and content while dealing with John's fickle whims. Even after breaking up, they had a comfortable, mutual adoration of each other. He deemed her proper and sweet and loved her, just not the way he loved Carlene. Instead, John admired Mary's morals. She was predictable and solid. Perhaps her best quality in his eyes was her infinite kindness to him and others. As for Mary, she had always openly admired John's idealism but had tepidly questioned his unbridled ambition. They loved each other, but there was no passion in it.

"Right, Mary, of course. And why? Because she adores you. And she's a teacher, too. Plus, she loves young children. Ideal, I tell you, she's ideal," Grudger said.

John's curiosity perked at the older man's interest. He asked, "Sam, have you ever been in love?"

"Sure thing, kid, hundreds of times. So many times, I forgot what real love is," he chuckled.

John persisted, "Do you think that passionate love is necessary for a partnership?"

Sam, endeared to John's optimistic view of romance, replied simply, "Passion is an asset, but it is not always ideal."

"Thanks, Sam," John concluded and hung up, pondering his friend's words.

The next day, John arose, fresh, determined, and surprisingly content. He decided to move forward, leaving his dreams with Carlene behind.

John drove to Open Grove Elementary School, where he'd attended school as a boy. The building was virtually the same. As John sat in his car, he fondly remembered his childhood and time at Open Grove. Full of carefree, happy days, with loving parents and kind and attentive teachers, Open Grove was a special space. The memories of his youth gave him a feeling of serene peace as he watched the parents and children go in and out.

The place he entered was unchanged, a return to a special place from a special time. John stopped by the office first to visit Dan Bowers, a former classmate of his and now the school principal.

"Congressman, wow, what an honor," Bowers boomed. "Our most famous alumnus ever came home."

"Hello, Dan. How are you? How's your dad?" John inquired. Bowers' dad had been principal thirty-five years before the young Bowers.

"Dad and I are doing great. He's still your biggest fan." The heir to Oak Grove continued, "How are you, John? Sad you left Congress?"

"No. Got a big deal brewing. I'll be fine, better than fine now."

Bowers shook his hand. "Best of luck, whatever it is." Bowers crossed his arms and bellowed admirably, "John Kinley, true statesman, wise scholar, and great American."

John merely said, "Thanks." However, he was startled by one of Bower's comments: "Great American." John felt the immediate question at hand: would he have to forfeit his American citizenship to begin his new endeavor? He was momentarily plagued by this dilemma but decided to address it later. For now, he had another plan. John asked Bowers if he could surprise Miss Jones with a visit.

Bowers eagerly accommodated him. "Sure! You know the way. Here's a hall pass—not that anyone would stop *you*, but it's the rules."

"Thanks," John said and left the office. Walking slowly down the halls, John was at peace. Its consistency was soothing, the rooms unchanged, and the lighting was all pleasingly the same. John had been a boy here. He'd dreamed of being a professional baseball player here. Flooded with memories and good feelings, John was glad to be back at Open Grove.

John approached Mary Jones' classroom and peered in. He saw Mary writing on an old chalkboard. *Wow!* he thought, *just like the old days—no sterile computers, just good old-fashioned learning.*

He eyed Mary briefly. She was petite and brunette but plain—pretty and attractive in a modest way. John did not want to startle her, so he knocked on the classroom door. Mary looked up as the handsome Kinley tentatively stuck his head into her domain.

"John! Come in, join the class," Mary said. Her tone was surprised but still kind and warm. Turning to her fourth graders, Mary said, "Class, this is John Kinley, our congressman."

"Former," he retorted.

"Yes," she amended, "former." The class gazed upon their visitor with eagerness. Not wanting to draw any more attention, John sat down and watched the remainder of the lesson without much ado. Mary, other than occasionally eyeing him, continued her lesson, which he deemed enjoyable.

The bell rang, the lesson ended, and Mary told the class, "Homework, class. Everyone read something happy, and be prepared to share it with us tomorrow. I want only happy endings for us all to enjoy." This was quintessentially Mary. John was pleased.

After the class departed, John and Mary hugged. John, always sure of himself with Mary, quipped, "Same old Mary."

"Old," she said with a pleasant laugh, "Really, John?"

"Old is good, Mary. It's predictable, stable, and grounded." The statesman was never at a loss for words with this long-time friend. He inquired, "School over for today?"

"Yes," she replied.

"Okay, let's go have an early dinner."

"Sure, anything you want. It's so good to see you and so soon after D.C."

They both knew where they were going to dinner without conferring: Bene's Pizza. Not only was it the best pizza in town, but John and Mary had spent many afternoons there together. It had become their spot. As always, John drove them to the restaurant, and Mary sat contentedly in his passenger seat, passing the time with light small talk. When they arrived, they happily entered the pizza parlor, John observing, "Wow, they never change; I love it."

The main dining space was spotted with small round tables, each topped with checkered tablecloths befitting the 1960s décor. John's dress shoes scuffed over the cheap hardwood as he led Mary to their usual table, a corner spot near the old, large pizza oven inlaid in the back wall.

He took Mary's coat, placed it over her chair, and they sat, making conversation easily. John told their usual waitress, "Sally, we are going to be here a while, a good, long while."

Neither John nor Mary drank alcohol, but they loved a local favorite soft drink, Crumley Cola, so John ordered a pitcher for them to share. Upon the arrival of the drinks, John, feeling especially buoyant, proposed a toast, "Here's to Crumley Cola, and here's to you, the best girl in the house."

Mary seemed flattered and smiled shyly.

After their second pitcher of the especially sweet, potent drink and some of Bene's finest pizza, John was relaxed, happy, and ready to get to his point. He looked at Mary and said, "Mary, I'm ready for a change, and you're it."

Surprised by the direct and bold comment, she smiled and whispered to him, "Wow, John. I knew leaving Congress would be a big deal for you, but I never thought it would include me." She cleared her throat and continued, "You must know, I would have gone to D.C. with you, or anywhere for that matter."

Hearing that, John looked into her eyes and smiled with a smugness he could only conjure up with Mary. "Glad you said that!" he proclaimed with a positive fist pounding on the table. "Then, you, my dear, will come with me."

"Come with you?" she inquired with hopeful trepidation. "Where?"

John met her eager gaze. Undaunted, he continued, eased by his limitless confidence with her, "Mary, do you trust me?"

"Yes," she replied.

"Do you love me?"

"Y-yes, John," she softly replied.

"You know I will always stand for the truth as an absolute, don't you?"

She nodded in quiet assent.

He continued, "Then, what I have to tell you is the truth; don't question it. Just listen, and then tell me yes, yes to everything."

Mary was puzzled but so in love with *her* statesman that she said, "I'm listening."

Pleased with his progress so far, John looked around. He noticed other patrons eavesdropping on their conversation.

"First," he said, "this calls for another pitcher of Crumley Cola!" She did not object, so he got another pitcher and poured it into fresh glasses.

Lowering his voice, John proceeded to explain every detail of his new venture to Mary: the terms, the place, the people, and the opportunity. He found himself now more of a salesman than Grudger had been, trying to convince Mary that he had made the right decision. Mary listened intently to John's seemingly fictional endeavor.

When Mary finally spoke, she appeared more serious than John had ever seen her before. "I'm not sure, John," she started. "This seems so unreal, farcical, fantastic in the sense of an imaginary dream. It just can't be so, not as you portray it."

John ignored her uneasiness and pressed her. "I need you. In fact, I'll marry you. How's that for starters?"

Mary smiled again for the first time in this phase of their discourse and, with her best attempt at humor, teasingly quipped, "So nice of you to ask and answer."

Mary looked doubtful, no doubt from years of his flighty behavior. To prove his feelings, John stood up, pulled her into his arms, and publicly kissed her. On-lookers fixated on the two lovers. Oblivious to them, John smiled, telling Mary, "Let's do it. I love you."

And he meant it. He knew their love was different than what he'd shared with Carlene, but it was sincere and stable.

Mary nodded, her lips curling into a timid smile. "I love you, too."

John had his First Lady, and Mary finally had John.

CHAPTER 6

The Founding of a Nation

John and Mary were wed at Saint Jude's, where John insisted his parish priest, Father Trew, perform the ceremony. It was just the three of them, simple and quick, accompanied by the faint smell of left-over incense, which clung to the empty wooden pews.

"Will we have a honeymoon?" Mary asked as the newlyweds left St. Jude's.

"Oh, yes," John replied, "a honeymoon for the ages. Let's take a flight."

Grudger was gone, out of the equation. He'd made the deal, taken his enormous fee, and moved on. However, John had received a text from Grudger's son, Al, letting him know that Al would be taking over relations between him and CBA. Al was fifty and a hustler's hustler, always looking for an angle, a deal. His father's son, but on the shifty side, with few of the elder's admirable qualities. John knew this but could not control this dynamic. John called Al and said, "Let's go. The ceremony is over, and I'm ready to travel. Let's do it."

The CBA plane picked up John, Al, and Mary and flew them to their new promised land. John felt emboldened while the other two wondered what lay ahead. The flight was long, ten, maybe twelve hours, but John's busy mind lost track of the minutes. Periodically, Mary quizzed John as the younger Grudger listened intently. "Where are we going? Where is this place?"

John was encouraging but purposefully vague in his responses. "Just wait and see. Everything will work out." He must have repeated that answer a dozen times during the flight.

Finally, the massive plane landed on a long, barren airstrip seemingly in the middle of nowhere, rolling to a bumping stop amidst the dense foliage. A simple trailer awaited John and Mary in a clearing not far from the airstrip. This would be their home until new lodgings could be constructed with the rest of their new nation.

Following John and Mary off the plane, Al, aglow with opportunity, stopped at the bottom of the boarding stairs and told them both, "Call me as you need things. Consider me a genie of sorts." He clearly did not plan to stay with them here in South America.

"Al," John said, "Are we safe?" Too many unanswered questions left John apprehensive in this foreign land. He glanced around, taking in the densely wooded area around the trailer, which emitted lively birdcalls.

"Safe is a relative term," Al said. "Get to work." Without further ado, he turned and walked up the stairs back into the plane, leaving John and Mary to their endeavor.

Over the next few weeks, John worked non-stop on his outlines—government, banks, military, schools, businesses, courts, and churches. *Ideals and ideas*, he thought. He was sovereign over an open domain. The book of his new state was blank, and John's will filled page after page. Unchecked and optimistic, he wrote and thought on. A trillion-dollar line of credit and one architect of statehood. How was he to accomplish this?

The food and furnishings in the trailer were modest and plain. John often worked with the windows open, letting in the fresh, rustic forest scent. Birdsong often accompanied his thoughts, sometimes mixing with the sound of Mary's gentle humming as she settled into their new home.

Neither John nor Mary complained as they began their lives together. They were newlyweds in the middle of nowhere, so it seemed. Their only visitor was the CBA plane, which periodically dropped off supplies.

John's focus was on parochial issues as he prepared plans for a new nation. He was free. Sovereign over no one and nothing yet except his ideas and dreams. John slept very little and awoke every day to write constantly, revising his notes and moving forward. John wanted to launch as soon as possible, but he yearned for perfection. After all, this was his ideal state, and the perfectionist in John's mind would not settle for the mundane. He wanted every aspect of this new nation to work according to his plan. Mary was quiet but always supportive. Her days were spent praying and supporting her husband in his novel endeavor. She cooked, cleaned, and queried John as to his progress and vision.

In a month, John proclaimed to Al Grudger that he was ready to launch. John had drafted the plans to bring forth his new nation, including its constitution, but he lacked one thing: a name. *What's in a name?* His country would be small, uninhabited, and, of course, new. That was it! Newland. Plain and simple, with an optimistic ring. Newland it would be. An English-derived name despite the locale in South America. John had no buildings yet and, hence, no place for printing presses or apparatuses, but he still needed a way to proclaim Newland's creation to the world. In preparation for the announcement, John told Al they would delegate their public relations to an outside source. Al agreed, as he did with every request or dictate, and began searching for the best firm money could buy.

Upon the arrival of New York's finest communications team, deemed the "No Names" by John, he told them abruptly to watch him, help him, and guide him. They were placed in newly constructed modest dwellings on-site next to John's trailer, and to John's satisfaction, they adjusted quickly to their basic accommodations. "Words will be to Newland," he told them as they settled in, "as crown jewels are to an empire—polished to perfection to gain the admiration of the world."

John recognized he needed help crafting his message, but he wanted the message to ring true. He wrote the very first press release to the world and quickly ran it by the "No Names," who offered minimal changes. He wrote, "Newland will be forged with the ideals of civilization past and present. Our goal is to glean everything positive from what was and is on this planet and to quell the negative traits of mankind." They were ready for the world.

The first international press conference was set for February 1. A podium was constructed on a small stage in an open field, and John was given a single, battery-powered microphone. Journalists came from all over the world, braving the jungle in quickly constructed, primitive abodes. The media pool in front of the podium swirled with skepticism, cynicism, and all the foibles of the news-mongering throngs. This was, of course, the birth of a new nation. On stage, John and Mary approached the podium.

"Welcome to Newland," John said. "Today, I address the international community. I'll be direct and brief." He paused to clear his throat and then continued, "This is a new nation, a small country with big dreams. As many of you know, I am an American. I served in its Congress. I love America and always will. However, I have been tasked with an interesting and almost incomprehensible endeavor to build a nation from inception to complete nation-state. I thank you for attending today. Citizens of the world, welcome to Newland. I have written a constitution, created the framework for a national bank, and begun a journey into the unknown."

The skeptical journalist corps took meticulous notes as the founder of Newland rambled on. "I will be inviting people from all over the world to join me through a special selection process. I want the world's finest; *we* want the world's finest. Allow me to provide a glimpse of our greatness as I can see and sense from your ennui that you are so far skeptical." John pressed on, blunt and forthright. "I have worked diligently to plan the start of our nation, and there are too many details to recite all at once, but I will do my best to give you a comprehensive vision of our nation. English will be our official language, but other tongues will be welcome. Christianity will be our official religion, with religious tolerance toward all. Newland will have the benefit of a virgin commencement with unlimited capital—monetarily and intellectually—and will launch with the fervor of unabated capitalism.

"These are just a few of our starting principles." He looked out among the press minions and said, "I'll take questions now."

As his eyes focused on the field of journalists, John recognized Sal Severin from the *New York Press*. "Hi, Sal," John felt at ease to see a familiar face. "A bit different from the Hill, huh?" he queried.

Severin, a jaded but honest professional, continued his career badgering of John in this new place. "John," he said, "What is this? What is this all about? How do you plan to grow, govern, and prosper? Whom or what deems this venture legitimate?"

Sensing the dogged negativity of Sal Severin, John leaned across the podium and confronted his old adversary, "Sal, you are a skeptic, a cynic. In this ideal state, optimism will propel results never before witnessed in history. It's like this: Wisdom, courage, and truth will guide us. Oh, and of course, God. We will have God to guide us, Sal. That's how I'll govern, and that's how I'll win."

Sal, grinning boldly, knew he had drawn John out and merely said, "That's quite the endorsement, Sovereign, or whatever you shall be called."

"Sovereign will be fine, Sal. I shall be Sovereign."

Sal looked disappointed to have failed to get a rise out of John. When he fell silent, the rest of the journalists peppered the nation's founder with a further array of general questions. John remained positive, steadfast, and undeterred. When the press event ended and the crowd disbursed, John went back to work more determined than ever.

Over the next few weeks, John transitioned from ideological founder to "Recruiter in Chief." He received resumes from all over the world, filling the trailer as he poured over the paperwork, searching for the elite, the best at and of everything, including engineers, doctors, researchers, and scholars.

While he toiled relentlessly, mobile trailers arrived daily, allowing a steady flow of goods to pour into the new nation. Al Grudger paid the bills from CBA's bountiful line of credit.

To John's surprise, international investors were offering Newland additional capital and investment opportunities despite the fledgling nature of the new state. Al, also pleasantly amazed by the interest in Newland, boasted on one of his short visits, "We're making a profit before we've even started. Dollars are flowing into this place. It's unbelievable!"

John, a bit perturbed by Al's glibness, exclaimed, "Al, this new nation is not a market or a commodity. It's a vision. We are in this experiment for the long haul, not a quick buck. Mind our fiscal house, and we will always have a stable home."

Al listened, grinned, and, minding his Sovereign, merely stated, "Got it, but the world is a commodity. I've seen it: ups, downs, highs, lows, profits, and losses. Pillars to plunder and rise to fall."

"We are better than that, bigger than that. We must be," John told him solemnly.

Undeterred by Al's cynicism, John continued to ponder the resumes, phone calls, and interest in Newland. So many people were offering their services and talents gratuitously for a chance to be part of an experiment in nation-building. Others were offering their talents for a price. In any event, demand was strong, and interest teeming. Newland was the talk of towns from New York to London, Paris to Moscow. John knew he had created a winner.

One night, John told Mary he had no idea that the events would move so swiftly. He needed a cabinet quickly. He set a date of March 1 for a convention to discuss the formal organization of the government of Newland. John secretly feared interest might wane if progress slowed down. He desperately needed assistance on all fronts. Luckily, John's boyhood friend, Kipp, had arrived in Newland a few days after the press conference.

Kipp was a follower to the core and loyal to a fault. He idolized John, and despite Kipp's sycophantic nature, John was glad to have an old friend at his side.

John insisted that his friend help him establish his new cabinet—not just any group of advisors, but a loyal, incorruptible, honest executive committee dedicated to the goals of Newland. Kipp told John that demand for a seat at this "Table of Triumph" was high, explaining, "The very best in the world want in. It's amazing. Leaders from all over the world are asking to get on board."

Kipp's first suggestion was Al Grudger, but John told Kipp, "Al is a mercenary. Mercenaries are fine on logistics but devoid of loyalty by definition. Render unto the mercenary that which he renders to the state. Use them as they would use us, nothing more, nothing less." Kipp agreed with John's assessment, and John thanked him.

John was overwhelmed by the international interest in his burgeoning endeavor. Newland was moving forward before the institutions of state or its personnel were in place. Without anyone to ease the burden of governance, John personally saw to it that roads were built, temporary housing was constructed, and food storage was emphasized. He ensured that infrastructure across the landscape was proceeding. Even without a formal government, abundant capital, talent, and efficiency propelled progress across and within the fledgling nation.

CHAPTER 7

The Convention

John put twelve trusted advisors and friends in his Supreme Cabinet, all of whom pledged their loyalty to John and Newland. He had some personal misgivings about the loyalty pledge and cautioned his Cabinet, "I appreciate your loyalty, but please remember, I always favor an oligarchy over a dictatorship. If the sovereign is just, wise, and sane, the latter is palatable for a short time. However, the human condition, which is prone to failures, sins, and foibles, dictates that governance by a class of committed citizens will ensure the survival of the state against a madman or corrupt sovereign."

The Cabinet members all agreed to move Newland toward an oligarchy.

March 1 arrived, a pivotal day in Newland's history. On that same simple airstrip that John and Mary had landed on only a few short weeks ago, now paved and extended, an aircraft arrived carrying one thousand volunteers. Private jets and other larger commercial jets crowded the runway, all containing Newland's precious cargo: their founding class. John and his Cabinet personally greeted every invitee. Their accommodations were modest temporary trailers like John's own, but all were committed to the success of the new nation.

The first thousand citizens of Newland were carefully screened before their arrival. John had recruited the brightest and best in many fields of expertise, commerce, and study. Most were dissatisfied Americans, but Europeans, Canadians, and citizens from every continent had representation. Al, of course, was present to observe the opening day festivities, checkbook in hand. Even he felt a sense of pride in Newland and the first group of its founding citizens despite his parochial self-interest.

John, feeling a bit tentative, had worked tirelessly on his cause. In preparation for their arrival, a constitution was finalized, and a flag proposal was drafted. John ensured that money was flowing easily from his enormous line of CBA credit, and investment dollars were still flowing in, to his surprise. A hastily constructed amphitheater would serve as the first Executive, Legislative, and Judicial venue for the time being. Despite this progress, John knew he needed more political structure, legal infrastructure, and direction.

John wanted his inaugural address to his fellow countrymen to be special. He entered the hastily constructed amphitheater dressed in a classic blue suit and red tie, similar to his attire on the Floor of the U.S. House. The Newlanders eagerly awaited his address, filling the seats in the plain room from wall to wall. His Cabinet of twelve, dressed in identical gray suits, also longed for the inception speech from their seats in the front row of the amphitheater. On a small, barren stage in the front of the room, John approached a bland podium with the Newland seal of state affixed to the front, complete with a bold bald eagle with sharp talons over a shape depicting the outline of Newland's borders. Above the seal was one word: Sovereign.

John's gaze scanned the crowd of diverse faces, a brain trust like no other ever assembled. Doctors, bankers, philanthropists, businessmen, and clergy were awaiting his official words. They were highly educated, affluent, and, in John's view, driven.

"Welcome to Newland," he stated plainly. "I am John Kinley."

Thunderous clapping echoed in the amphitheater. "By trade, I am a lawyer, thinker, and former American politician, and now, I endeavor to found, with you, an ideal state." He paused. "*The* Ideal State."

Again, applause erupted.

"Together, we have the capital intellectually and financially to start anew. Many of you have, like me, come from other countries, always wondering, 'Is there more? Is there something better? Is there a way to build, govern, live, and flourish differently from the inherited constraints of our respective former homelands?' Each and every one of you, our founders, are bright, successful, and well-educated in your fields of expertise. Most importantly, you must be incorruptible in your governing, service, business, or any undertaking you may pursue. This is essential, and our purpose must always be to do what is best for the majority of Newlanders based on the true facts and circumstances facing the nation.

"Newland will be a strong state. Honest, proud, and patriotic. It is far better to conceive a nation in truth, even when the truth trumps values and virtues that some deem admirable. We will be a nation of immigrants. Legal immigrants, of course—selected, coveted, legal invitees to a nation of law, order, and success. I will be Newland's first Sovereign, but I alone cannot solve every problem and surmise every solution. Nonetheless, I promise you and the world, which is watching, that my life and my being shall be wholly dedicated to God and Newland."

The applause following this declaration was deafening. Settling the crowd, John continued, "Think long and hard before you commit, for I will be Sovereign. I will govern with advice from a few as an oligarchy of sorts, but all final decisions shall rest with me. My word will be law, my decisions not appealable at first. But alas, I, too, am mortal and limited in perpetual scope. With an eye toward the future of this new great nation, I pledge to be a benevolent sovereign, but any nation-state must guard against the idiotic, corrupt, unjust, or tyrannical despot. Oligarchy should be our ultimate form so that our goals of truth, honor, dignity, success, and exceptionalism shall not perish after my sovereignty but may, in fact, flourish for eons to come if the right people govern.

"It is with a heart and mind for justice and a will to forge a nation never seen by the planet that I will lead. As Sovereign—make no qualms about it—I shall be omnipotent. I am unabashed in my ideology that democratization and trends to dilute the wealth and power of the ruling class ultimately fuel the erosion and destruction of any body politic and, hence, the people they serve. But I cannot deny that human rights are inalienable and come from God. It is for this reason we will live under a grand social contract ceding some rights to a strong Sovereign for the benefit of all. Together, we shall lead; together, we shall serve. For all who are with me, you have granted me your sovereignty. I promise you that we shall stock the annuls of history with an inventory of greatness. Through us, mankind will triumph over evil and challenge human maladies. Our values will be timeless. Historians who are not demented by deception but who search for truth and the survival of our species will someday deem us an ideal state for the ages. Join me, join us, and join our destiny for greatness with your oath of allegiance."

The crowd roared, erupting again in a newfound fervor. There was no dissent present. John led the thousand as a whole in their oath of allegiance. The international onlookers who had been invited to observe this momentous event were amazed. Seeing this, John was very pleased with himself. He had been sincere, strong, and forthright.

Turning to his twelve and Mary seated beside them, he declared, "I am Sovereign now. Let us show the world who we are."

Finally, John looked over at Al Grudger. Sitting in the front row next to Mary, Al was agog by the emotional outpouring dedicated to the rookie leader. Al smiled in a way eerily similar to that of his father and flashed ten fingers to the new ruler of Newland. That was his commission—ten percent of everything. John just nodded his assent, and they disbursed.

Chapter 8

The Newland Constitution

The Preamble

The People of the State of Newland, in order to form an ideal state, establish truth above all to protect the prosperity of the nation. In this way, the People, under one Sovereign, establish this Constitution for Newland.

Article I

Section 1

The powers of the state shall be divided among three branches, including legislative, executive, and judiciary.

Section 2

The executive branch, led solely by the Sovereign, maintains broad authority to make law and policy by executive decree under the condition that it is published for the public, maintaining truth as the highest value.

Section 3

The legislative branch will be led by a Supreme Cabinet, made up of twelve advisors who are subject to change by edict of the Sovereign, which shall have the power to enact laws and appropriations for the good of the people.

Section 4

The legislative branch shall also contain a Congress made
up of two distinct chambers, the Senate and the House,
and shall have voting powers, but their laws, rules, and
resolutions are advisory. The Sovereign alone holds the
power to institute or veto such legislation. Members of
the House shall be elected to two-year terms, unlimited.
The Senate shall be appointed by the executive branch
for a six-year term.

Section 5

The judicial branch shall be led by the High Court, which shall
be made up of nine justices serving at the discretion of the
Sovereign, who may strictly interpret the laws but shall not
go beyond this function.

Article II

Section 1

The Sovereign shall hold absolute power over the Army, Navy,
Airforce, and Sovereign Guard as the Commander in
Chief.

Section 2

A Vice Sovereign shall be appointed to chair the Senate as
Sovereign of the Senate. The Vice Sovereign may succeed
the Sovereign only in the event of the Sovereign's death,
followed in succession by the Speaker of the House and
the Chief Justice of the High Court.

Section 3

Statements of Affirmation may be created by the Sovereign to
protect individual liberties and ensure the protection of
fundamental rights.

Section 4

The Sovereign may invoke Sovereign Law in cases of rebellion
or invasion, as public safety may require it.

Article III

Section 1

The Newland press shall be controlled by the Office of Sovereign
Communications, chaired by a member of the Supreme
Cabinet.

Section 2

The search for truth shall always outweigh the right to privacy.
For this reason, a warrant is not necessary for search and
seizure.

Section 3

All tax-paying citizens over the age of eighteen may vote,
regardless of race, gender, or religious affiliations.

Section 4

There shall be no federal income tax on wages or investments.
Sales tax and floating national tariffs are acceptable.

Section 5

Newland shall be a safe haven for Jews. Every Jewish person is
entitled to citizenship and a safe haven that is equal to the
rights bestowed by the Jewish State.

The international reaction to the published constitution was
mixed. Many Western democracies, including the United
States, were critical and demeaning. In fact, the *New York
Press* described the constitution as "a sham document for a
sham nation, run by a sham politician deemed Sovereign." Most

countries and their press deemed Newland too small and insignificant to comment upon. But by this time, Russia and China had decided to try to curry favor with the new nation and its new leader if for any reason to aggravate the United States and its criticism of Newland.

John dismissed the criticism. He told the international press, "Our critics refuse to recognize Newland, yet declare us a foe. All is well in Newland." John and Newland had made friends, foes, naysayers, and skeptics before the ink was dry on its constitution. Nonetheless, John was pleased with his governing document. It was open to revision by him and him alone, with or without the approval of the legislature or Courts. Since Newland was so small in geography and population, it did not have a federalist system. Local government would be superfluous, and state government impossible.

John was not only pleased; he was reinvigorated every day, nay every hour, with a push toward more, always more: more order, more prosperity, more nationalism. Newland, his ideal state, had sprung from virgin land and now had a script in place to lead it forward.

Chapter 9

Growing Pains

Newland's first year saw some interesting challenges. The new, albeit subservient, legislature was teeming with optimism and eager to endorse the pro-growth, pro-capital projects and laws of the Sovereign. Unity was not only a key virtue in Newland but the dominant mood. Leadership was quick to quell debate beyond the mere scope of inquiry, and serenity was abounding in Legislative Newland. The judiciary was equally as vibrant and accommodating, accepting the Sovereign's penal and commercial codes with enthusiasm. Justice was based on truth, and punishment, although severe, was dedicated to the goal of deterrence.

John was pleased with his complimentary branches as they developed their roles in Newland. Constitutionally, John had created a mechanism to test his edicts with the High Court before he made them. The Supreme Cabinet swiftly and emphatically affirmed his dictates with advisory opinions, glowing with praise for its executive.

Overall, John was enjoying his role as an absolute ruler. He still feared an absolute sovereign other than himself, shuddering at the prospect of a future corrupt, vile, or incompetent leader. John, perhaps naively, still believed a transition to a true republic was possible in the future. But, his steadfast opposition to a true democracy and his passionate abhorrence to any form of egalitarian ventures kept him committed to his leadership structure.

John wanted his people to create wealth and productive work, for the ability to earn, grow, and accumulate individual wealth was key to the Ideal State. Individual and corporate philanthropy was championed as well. The national sales tax was not only successful but was also the cornerstone of Newland's insistence that all citizens must pay taxes consistent with their consumption and not their ability to earn. The tax structure, especially the legal ban on income taxes, created a boom in all aspects of Newland's economy.

In its very first year, infrastructure grew and corporations hatched and prospered all across Newland. Construction crews covered the city, and cranes littered the skyline. Aesthetically pleasing buildings of brick and concrete sprung up like weeds, forming a well-planned, carefully structured urban setting. The hustle and bustle of new construction permeated the air from dawn until dusk, the scent of diesel fumes and freshly poured concrete ever-present. Free enterprise abounded in a way the world had never seen before.

The absence of any major environmental code propelled new growth and expansion. In its place, the citizens of Newland seemed to develop a self-imposed environmental plan. Environmental laws did not need to dictate how they were to build, prosper, and grow. Instead, natural law governed their ventures, as their sovereign often shared the views of Renaissance philosophers with his new nation, professing their belief of how the orderly structure of the universe is reflected in the laws of nature. This created a national sense of pride in protecting the environment. It was part of Newland's nationalistic psyche. All over the world, nations began to take note of Newland's experiment in unbridled capitalism—an experiment that was successful to date with no end in sight.

As the need for laborers increased, they were accepted into Newland on work visas. Workers eagerly came to Newland in droves. Truly exceptional workers or those with special skills could apply for a long-term chance at citizenship. Unions were outlawed in the Constitution with a prohibition on minimum wage laws as well. The Commerce Department of Newland, under John's watchful eye, monitored economic progress and the labor force in Newland.

Despite the boundless optimism in Newland, the pains of rapid growth took their toll on infrastructure, government agencies, and the citizenry of the new nation. The country was under constant pressure for progress. As hospitals and schools were constructed, filling jobs continued to be a difficult task. John, a micro-manager-in-chief, monitored his agencies and data with meticulous scrutiny. The government was growing, too, with agencies adding personnel at a tremendous pace. The traditional bureaucrat was not a creature of Newland. From clerk to Cabinet member, service was a calling, not a curse.

Regardless of the employer, public or private, service to Newland was the driving force behind workers' willingness to perform at higher levels. Posters adorned most workplaces with heroic pictures of workers in their chosen field, underlined with the slogan "Always Strive For More!"

The system worked efficiently, and corrections were made swiftly, often without question or comment. Results mattered in every sector. John had said time and time again that mediocrity would not be part of Newland's vocabulary, and he meant it.

As the New Year approached in Newland, John summoned his Cabinet and communications advisors to the newly completed, state-of-the-art Sovereignty Building. To celebrate, or rather, to communicate to the world that it was Newland's anniversary, he wanted to give an ornate State of the Nation Address. His goal, despite the obvious acclaim he sought for Newland, was the truth. He wanted to honestly portray Newland to the world after one year of development. In his meeting with his Cabinet, he demanded truthful answers and truthful statistics, and he cautioned them not to provide the nation and the world with anything but honest, provable numbers.

The nation's anniversary date arrived. John awoke in their newly built but still humble Sovereign residence and looked over at Mary, smiling confidently. Mary gleamed back at John with an eternal look of love. John, it seemed, was clearly more excited about Newland's anniversary than his own a few weeks earlier, but Mary understood. Her love for him had grown and was unyielding. And in turn, despite the relentless overtures of many beautiful, powerful, and successful women over the last year, John had happily remained loyal. Mary's unending support was a constant comfort, and every day since arriving in Newland, John's appreciation and love for her progressed. Loyalty had come easily with such a loving and supportive companion. John loved Mary, and his only mistress was Newland. The new nation controlled him as much as he controlled it. As John arose gleefully, Mary stopped him and said with a smile, "Take care of Newland, John. It's her anniversary today."

Later, over breakfast, John sat at their small dining table with Mary and told her about his State of the Nation Address. She listened intently as he went over the accomplishments of their first year.

When he finished, Mary inquired shyly, "May I join you at your speech tonight?"

"Of course," he replied gladly, "I have a seat up front for you."

As he got up to leave, Mary stopped him, speaking in a hesitant tone, "Before you leave this morning, can I have a brief chat with you?"

Surprised, John said, "Yes, but quickly, please. Today, I am going to cement our place in history. One year of Newland, our State, our dream, our destiny." He realized that he had done just about all of the talking during their breakfast together, but he could not contain his enthusiasm as he proceeded to tell her, "The world is full of skeptics, naysayers, and people bent on criticizing others. Today, we will address them head-on with veracity and candor, informing them of our progress. We are going to be the envy of the world." After realizing he *still* had not let Mary speak, John apologized, "Sorry, I'm getting carried away. It's just that we are doing so well, better than I imagined, better than even our most ardent supporters had hoped."

Mary stood up and with a loving hug, looked into John's eyes and said, "I'm going to have a baby."

John forgot his rant about Newland. He'd never even fathomed she could or would be pregnant. "Wow," he said in a quiet whisper, "Mare, this is great!"

Tears welled up in her eyes as he returned her hug. "A First Child of Newland!" he exclaimed. "Don't worry. We have the best doctors here. They've come from all over the world. No malpractice claims, high salaries, and they will be at your beck and call. I will make sure that they treat you like the gem you are."

Though she was happy to share the good news, Mary felt a bit like one of Newland's positive statistics. John's rhetoric was predictable. His ideal state was about to add another accomplishment: a First Child. Of course, this new asset pleased John.

Chapter 10

The Address

John approached the Chamber of the People's House in his newly constructed Sovereignty Building. It was clean, bright, and designed to mirror the promise of all that was Newland, with Roman-inspired architecture, imposing columns, and ornate gold molding. The chamber was filled with the House, Senate, Judicial, and military leaders. For the event, his Cabinet members dressed alike in the same suits, ties, and even the same functional but proper black shoes. Order and efficiency were the goals of the day, and the governing class of Newland was present, ready, and eager to hear from their Sovereign. For John, this seemed all too reminiscent of the American State of the Union Address, which he had attended out of a sense of duty for four years. John yearned for something different.

Everyone in the gallery was ticketed and carefully selected for the anniversary address by the Office of Communications. Even the press, especially the international press, was screened to the best of the agency's ability. Foreign leaders, ambassadors, and Newland's domestic press had prime seating. Newland's press corps, or as John affectionately referred to them as his "Fifth Estate," were ready to perform their assigned tasks.

John was pleased to observe the Chamber, filling to overflow capacity as his leaders paraded down the aisles to their seats. The festivities began when Mary entered the chamber to thunderous applause. Mary was popular in Newland; her humble approach to being First Lady and her commitment to education made her endearing to the populace. The Newland anthem, patriotic but tasteful, flowed from speakers around the Chamber, prodding the Chamber attendees to rise respectfully. John waited by a Chamber door near the front of the room, watching the scene and sensing the moment. As the anthem progressed, he briskly thrust himself into the Chamber and walked the short distance to the podium at the front. The audience stood in unabated applause. The anthem ended with a bombastic crescendo, seemingly atypical for the relatively moderate tune. The line "Ever Newland, always Newland" concluded the anthem, and the Sovereign waited for the applause to wane. Finally, the Chamber sat and grew silent, and John was ready to begin. He glanced over his shoulder at several members of the Sovereign Guard, an elite military group created by John for the sole purpose of protecting the Sovereign. The Guard stood alert, their eyes missing nothing.

John, swelling with pride, allowed the emotion to run rampant through the Chamber. He opened his mouth to speak, but the Chamber erupted again with a seemingly endless ovation. John nodded in approval. The crowd began an unscripted chant of "Sovereign!" which rumbled through the large space. The booming, thunderous chant was especially pleasing to John. He was Sovereign, Newland was his, and Newland's first birthday would be a resounding success. An indescribable emotion began to rise in him. He was so moved. He began to tremble due to the exuberance he felt.

John began anew, "Thank you, thank you."

"Sovereign!" continued to ring out.

"Please, please," John pleaded with the throngs of admirers, acutely aware that the international press was watching and covering his every move. "My fellow countrymen, a year ago, we began a journey—a voyage unlike any endeavor the world has ever seen. I committed to founding a nation-state the likes of which has never been experienced or witnessed by mankind. I report to you today that the state of Newland is ideal in formation, in reality, and in all that we do and all that we are."

John continued his speech, detailing the growth of Newland's economy, infrastructure, education, healthcare, and trade. His figures were direct and accurate, meticulously detailing every aspect of Newland's current economic status. Statistic after statistic, goal after goal, these accomplishments of staggering growth were not only rhetoric but also the reality in Newland.

After an hour, John concluded with his dogmatic reverence for the truth, "What I extolled to you today is true. Every fact and figure. We must, however, do more. It is the inherent condition of humankind to fall prey to decadence, even within the best nation-states. We will not rest on our laurels. In Newland, we are ever striving to develop potential, minimize the sins of mankind, fix mistakes, and move forward, ever forward."

After the speech, members filed out, following their Sovereign. Despite the audience's accolades for the Ideal State and their leader's professed accomplishments, a sense of exhaustion filled the Chamber. The exalted show of approval had emotionally drained even the most casual observers, of which there were few.

Most of those in attendance came away even more impressed with Newland than before the disclosure of its first annual statistics. Despite the local and national acclaim for

Newland, the most important accomplishment to John was the international media coverage of the event. In one year, the international press had moved from editorials of farce and fantasy to at least tacit recognition. Of course, the conservative state received more criticism from the international press due to the new nation's abhorrence of any liberal notions of governance. From the nation's inception, every pro-growth, pro-capitalism, pro-business endeavor had been attacked voraciously by the now awe-struck press. Newland's success was anathema to the international fourth estate. Notwithstanding this fact, John had finally received the attention, if not respect, of the world.

John was very pleased. His speech was brutally honest about the nation's progress, relying on sound facts and a good record. When asked for his commentary on the anniversary, he said two things, "Newland is a real, financially sound nation-state with boundless aspirations—and its Sovereign is popular." John emphasized that he was more popular among his populace than any other leader in the world. He told the press, "That's not just hubris; it's the truth."

Although Mary was supportive throughout the event, she was disappointed that John had failed to mention their child's impending birth. When she asked him about it later that night, he had the Office of Communications prepare a press release, which they released the next day. It was concise, positive, and without fanfare.

Chapter 11

All Sectors Ahead

The next day, still aglow in light of the anniversary and the international attention, John called a Cabinet meeting, hoping to savor their success a little longer. In addition to his twelve standing Cabinet members, he'd invited a thirteenth member to the meeting: Hinkins, the newly appointed Commander of the Sovereign's Guard.

As a former American Special Operations Officer, Hinkins's resume was impressive. Six foot three, strong, confident, and endowed with piercing eyes, he was stoic but fiercely loyal, stern, and unwavering. Hinkins, though German by birth, was a student of military history who copiously studied the history of Rome. In his view, Caesars had their praetorians; John would have his Sovereign Guard. Hinkins came into the Cabinet meeting dressed in military black, four stars adorning his shoulders.

John, a lover of history, had always been enamored by the Roman Empire. In a subtle way, John saw Newland as an extension of the once-great empire and its institutions. To John, Hinkins represented a Praetorian figure of the Sovereign's realm. All of Newland was loyal to the Sovereign, but the Sovereign's Guard took a special oath of loyalty to John and John alone.

Hinkins's presence at the Cabinet meeting sent ripples of discomfort around the Chamber, as the new member's uniform of solid black from head to toe stood starkly different than the prim and unvarying business attire of the Cabinet. Nevertheless, Hinkins was welcomed. When it was Hinkins' turn to address his new peers in front of his Sovereign, he touted the Sovereign Guard's devotion to Newland's Head of State and Head of Government. "Unyielding loyalty is imperative to protect our Sovereign," Hinkins stressed, informing the Cabinet members of five hundred elite members who had just finished their Guard training, each driven by such loyalty.

John had ordered Hinkins to grow the Guard, but slowly and with an emphasis on quality. They were to be Newland's Supermen. The Cabinet, though not lackeys by nature, had become de facto lackeys in practice and applauded the Commander of the Sovereign Guard at the conclusion of his remarks. Smitten with Kinley's persona, the ministers were convinced that such a guardian of the Sovereign would be beneficial to Newland.

The Cabinet meeting continued, with John's thirteen ministers gathered around their new round table. Each Cabinet post was a cherished and coveted seat, each person selected by John as Sovereign and approved unanimously by the Senate. No one had resigned since his or her seating, and there had been no removals.

John asked each Cabinet member to give an in-depth update on their respective department, including finances, status, personnel, plans, goals, and outlook. Other members were free to make recommendations, but only John could approve or direct final action. Amazingly, Cabinet meetings to date had occurred without negativity. Suggestions were taken or rejected with an ease of politeness. The etiquette of Newland's ruling class was acquiescence, with each Cabinet member attempting to out-manner the next with the compliments of the State. John relished the atmosphere of unity.

As the Cabinet meeting came to a close, John turned to his Minister of Commerce and his Minister of Education. He boldly announced, "I want Newland to have a grand hotel and an outstanding university. Not necessarily in that order, but perhaps to be constructed concurrently. My resolve is to have this accomplished in very short order for the grandeur of Newland."

The Minister of Tourism, Sands, chimed in, "Sovereign, consider it done. Say where and when."

John responded without hesitation, "Capitol City, right in the middle of Capitol City."

Growth in Newland was planned and structured around Capitol City and was expected to gradually expand outward over time. Despite Newland's limited size, there was still ample room for growth and expansion due to the work of its world-class city planners. Before Versal, the Minister of Education, could comment on the request for a university, Sands replied, "Sovereign, Capitol City it will be. I'll have the plans within six months, and construction can begin two months after that."

John looked Sands over but did not comment. His hesitation prompted the ever-pleasing Sands to rebid for his Sovereign's approval. "Plans in three months, construction to start in one?"

"Much better," John told Sands, "This project is special to me. Understand that it must be second to none and reflect the grandeur of Newland."

Baffled by John's insistent tone, Sands attempted to lighten the discussion and quipped, "The Sovereign Hotel."

Missing the humor in Sand's comment, John readily agreed to the quip and responded, "Great idea!"

John then turned his attention to the quiet and reserved Versal. At eighty, Versal was John's oldest Cabinet minister. As a former professor of liberal arts, scholar, writer, and thinker, John highly valued Versal's input and felt he was a very capable Minister of Education. Versal was well-read, well-taught, and a gifted teacher. In order to lure Versal to Newland, John had him declared Professor Emeritus and Poet Lauriat of Newland. The latter title John had wished to reserve for himself. He'd ceded this title to woo his favorite professor, and it had worked. "Versal," John said, "We need a great university, a university to rival the greatest academic institutions in the world. Build it and staff it. We have the resources, Professor, to attract and retain the very best." John pressed Versal further, "I want capitalists, ardent capitalists—*no socialists on the faculty*. Versal, I expect you to deliver. Are you able to handle that?"

Versal, an independent thinker, inquired further, "Sovereign, may I be so bold as to ask you some questions?"

John admired Versal's intellect and displayed a unique tolerance toward him. So, to the amazement of his other ministers, John replied, "Please, Versal, speak freely and without fear. I solicit your thoughts. A good and decent Sovereign must listen to opposing views from time to time. This is not a sign of weakness but a sign of humility. So long as the Sovereign can make the absolute final decision, opposing views can and should be presented to any good leader. As Sovereign, I, too, am human. I, too, am limited in my abilities and am subject to error."

Versal stood up and addressed John as a mentor would a student. With a candid and respectful tone, he began,

"Sovereign, if an exclusive group of capitalists aligned with the American conservative party is your wish for our faculty, consider it done. If I may, I suggest at least one or two politically moderate professors at the University. I, too, do not want any hardened socialists, as they are a blemish not only upon the body politic but also on the recipients of their dogma, the students. Diversity, though, might be welcomed to provoke some form of individual, independent thinking. In fact, Sovereign, it might embolden the students to embrace our philosophy in a more potent way."

John thought deeply, albeit briefly, and exclaimed, "Versal, do it. Build it and staff it, but be careful. This must be a world-class university. I will rely and depend on you."

Pleased with his Sovereign's attempt at flexibility, Versal said, "I shall begin at once."

Hearing from the rest of his Cabinet ministers, John was pleased to learn that the respective sectors of the Newland economy were growing; agriculture, commerce, education, workforce development, health, military, communications, transportation, infrastructure, and athletics were improving, with more progress planned for the future. On this hopeful note, the meeting came to a close.

Two weeks after their meeting, Sands personally delivered the plans for The Sovereign Hotel. Striding into John's office with abundant pride, Sands said, "Sovereign, here are the plans. The hotel will be magnificent!"

Though pleased with Sands' obedience to the schedule, John made himself very clear, "Only the best, you understand?" Before Sands could answer, John pressed on, "I want, no, I demand nothing less. Foreign travelers have stayed in trailers, huts, and sometimes tents as we developed. I want to make a statement about us, about Newland. This hotel will be that vehicle."

Sands timidly replied, "Yes, Sovereign. I understand. The plans propose a grand hotel, but I must confess, sir, it's not unique."

Shaking his head with disapproval, John snapped, "No, that is not good enough! We have architects, engineers, and designers. Fix it. Newland demands the exceptional."

Stammering, Sands merely said, "Yes, s-sir. Right away."

"Good," John responded. "So, where exactly is the site?"

"It's in the middle of Capitol City, on Main Street at the far end of the Plaza of Lights."

John was pleased for a brief moment and then pressed, "Next week, you and I will go over the rules for the new hotel."

"Rules, sir?" Sands inquired.

John replied, "Yes, Sands, the complete set of rules for the hotel."

Wrenching his hands in confusion, Sands stammered again, "Yes, s-sir. I understand." They shook hands, and Sands hurriedly exited to begin anew.

Chapter 12

Al

The abundance of readily available capital, both domestically and from foreign investment, resulted in booming growth in Newland. Businesses were easy to create and nurture. Newland, as a sovereign entity, maintained complete control of its real estate portfolio. It employed every tool imaginable to grow, develop, and promote this resource. Projects sprung up and were, for the most part, immensely successful. Problems and issues were resolved swiftly by department heads, always with the goal of growth and a slant toward profit.

Al Grudger continued to profit handsomely and was candidly and openly impressed with Newland's rapid and continued success. He, like his father before him, admired and had an appreciation for John, but his heart and soul were committed to himself. Despite his mercenary bent, Al was actually beginning to believe in the dream of Newland as business after business arose from nothing with no perceivable end in sight.

Al roved from one deal to another, gleaning commissions from every transaction that enriched Newland. This morning, he sat down for his appointment with the Minister of Commerce to review the nation's fiscal status. Al was astonished as he perused Newland's books. Newland's economy and net worth had grown substantially from its initial trillion-dollar start-up.

Astonished by Newland's progress, which was far beyond what he could have imagined, Al praised the minister and pushed for more details. He found that the nation's assets had multiplied and doubled its net worth in slightly more than a year's time. After reviewing Newland's astonishing numbers, Al requested a meeting with John.

Al Grudger could visit anywhere with an apparent "carte blanche," including meeting with the seemingly infallible Sovereign in the modest office he maintained in the Sovereignty Building. Al referred to John by name and not as Sovereign. This was acceptable to John, as while he had grown used to the fawning nature of most of his countrymen, he valued Al's independence. Al was polite to John and, at times, even jovial but never in awe of him. John readily accepted Al's many visits, deeming his honesty beneficial.

Al entered John's office, shook his hand, and sat at the desk across from John. "It's been a good run so far."

John nodded. "Al, when your father made me this offer, I wondered, 'How? Why?' But we have built growth, prosperity, and international respect." Al leaned forward with keen intent. John continued, "I'm thrilled, even a bit amazed."

Al nodded with a sincere smile at the Sovereign, saying, "I am impressed and thrilled for you as well."

With Al's praise, John felt compelled to articulate his success and vision. "Al, we have just begun. In a little more than one year, we have attained the unattainable."

"You live for this, don't you?" Al said with a knowing smile.

"Yes, of course I do. It's my state, my vision. Of course, I live for Newland." John grasped Al's hands and looked right into his eyes. Stern, serious, and bold, he declared, "This experiment could be an empire."

Al was skeptical. "An empire? Surely, a country barely the size of Delaware can't be an empire."

John stared at Al with firm resolve. "Watch us, Al," John said. "Watch me. I lay awake at night, always thinking. I dream awake during the day." Al listened intently as John continued. "We make history every day and expect more the next day. Why not an empire? The world is filled with mediocrity. Mediocre countries and mediocre leaders, all wandering through history as icons of nothingness. They are often replaced without notice. They fail, they squander, and even if they languish through the eras, they define insignificance."

Al knew then that John was more driven, more determined than ever. He was bent on a vision of Newland's supremacy that neither Al nor his father envisioned. Al wondered if the sovereign leader would continue to prosper or if his vision of greatness would bring them all to ruin. At present, Al was satisfied to accede to John's plans and enjoy the prosperous ride for as long as it lasted.

Al stuck his hand out and merely said, "It's up to you, John. You know I am my father's son. I don't care what you do so long as the money keeps flowing in."

John beamed back at Al, saying, "I've never tried to deprive you of a dollar. But in my view, you are brokering Newland's greatness for a price. Let me be clear: I am not angry about your goals; mine are just different. Newland is prospering, and it's better than I could have imagined. When I set forth principles on which to build this place, I did not imagine it could be this good. Think about it: a nation of constant growth and patriotism—without crime, I might add—that is grander than I've ever witnessed anywhere else."

Al impishly smiled, appearing amused by John's candid tone. Filled with confidence anew, John felt a desire to profess to Al, "Our people have good jobs. They are secure and live without fear. There was something different and special about those three men who visited me with your father. They must have known something I didn't, something far-reaching and incredible."

Al, for the first time, grew a bit ashen. He quietly murmured, "Maybe they still know more than us."

John found his remark puzzling and replied quickly, "What do you mean, 'Know more than us'? The CBA never calls. Your father has moved on. There have been no visits or comments from our benefactors. Surely, Al, they are pleased?"

Al, wishing to leave the subject, replied, "Perhaps we will hear from them in the near future."

John nodded and said, "Until then, we shall move forward, ever forward."

Chapter 13

The Visit

Newland continued to boom in every way possible. Growth, profit, investment, and legal immigration flourished as scholars, professionals, and entrepreneurs flowed into Newland by the thousands. The country's infrastructure continued to expand to accommodate the population boom. The sound of construction crews was an ever-present din in the background of Newland's urban life.

International skeptics had been silenced; the initial success of Newland was undeniable. Critics did, however, chide the burgeoning State with complaints about the inequities in wealth, lack of civil liberties, and the Sovereign's apparent omnipotent reign. The choice to sacrifice many personal liberties commonly found in Western democracies in exchange for security and deference to the Sovereign was often questioned by journalists. However, John not only accepted criticism from international liberals, but he also relished it. John taunted his critics by flaunting the causes that riled them. His exaltation of Newland was constant in Newland's press and all its institutions.

The Sovereign Hotel had sprung up faster, better, and more opulent than planned, adorned with the Newland flag and food to rival the world's finest restaurants. The grand opening was set for the first of June. It was far from the rudimentary start of his nation-state with its primitive kickoff on dirt mounds. This hotel was Newland's crowning achievement to date. There were so many requests to attend the grand opening of the hotel that the Minister of Tourism, Sands, had to ask John to personally choose the guest list. Rain checks for later dates were issued in abundance so as not to disappoint inquiring tourists. John wanted the world to see and appreciate Newland, and the Sovereign Hotel would be his flagship for the tour.

Long before the grand opening, rooms were booked with restaurant reservations abounding. Rules were boldly declared to all guests upon their arrival. The cans and can'ts at the Sovereign Hotel were carefully scripted and agreed to in advance, including a strict adherence to moderation, politeness, and mutual hospitality. The Sovereign Hotel, like so much of Newland's infrastructure, was fully paid for. The trillion-dollar investment in Newland had now tripled and continued to grow. The hotel was an ever-present reminder of the nation's economic progress. John was so pleased with the results obtained by Sands that he ordered him to begin construction of a second hotel called La Verdad to honor Newland's steadfast commitment to honesty.

Two days prior to the grand opening of The Sovereign Hotel, Sands met with John to finalize the plans. Sands entered John's office and was greeted by two Sovereign Guards. Tall, stern, and ever loyal to their leader, they awaited John's reaction. When John smiled at Sands and motioned for him to take a seat, the guards sat in quiet reverence to their leader, ever observant and solicitous of the Sovereign's every whim. John praised Sands aloud to his two special guards. "This, gentleman, is our distinguished Minister of Tourism. The genius behind the Sovereign Hotel."

"Thank you, Sovereign," Sands said.

John inquired, "Are we ready to go, Sands?"

Excitedly, Sands replied, "Yes, Sovereign. The best of everything for you, sir. I have read, studied, and applied your rules to every aspect of the hotel. I understand your adherence to moderation and the rules. They will be implemented to the letter, sir."

"You represent everything good about Newland: thrift, honesty, success, and achievement." John chuckled and told his Minister, "You can stop me anytime."

Sands was silent.

John then asked, "Any other issues, Minister?"

Sands hesitated before replying, "Sovereign, I have a request—a dilemma of sorts. May I speak freely?"

The Sovereign Guards perked up at this candid discourse.

"Sure. Go ahead; speak freely. I am a just and fair Sovereign. You have proved your loyalty and success with the hotel. Speak freely."

Sands stood erect. "Sovereign, I want every aspect of the opening to be a perfect reflection of the hard work of Newland."

"Of course. We've gone over that, and I'm pleased," John said. "What's up?"

Sands took a deep breath. "Sir, a request has been made—a very late request—to attend the opening of the Sovereign Hotel. We are not only full with a massive waiting list, but this lady called three times and insisted that I appeal to you for a room and a place at the ceremony."

A bit perplexed by Sands' apparent inability to deal with a very routine task, John replied, "Sands, you have designed, constructed, and orchestrated one of the best hotels in the world;

surely, you can handle a few declinations on reservations. If we are full, we're full."

Sands progressed in a sincere but bumbling manner. "Sir," he said, "it's a Carlene LeFaze."

John froze.

Sands continued, "She says she's known you well for a long time. This isn't the first time I've gotten a call like this but she was different; she's demanding and persuasive. What should I do?"

John, now the uneasy orator in the conversation, murmured, "Carlene . . . really?"

The Sovereign Guards saw an uneasiness in their Sovereign that they had not witnessed to date. John was flustered by the news. Again, he murmured, "Wow, Carlene."

Sands awaited John's instructions in perfect silence. In fact, the room grew utterly still for over a minute while John pondered his next order.

Finally, he spoke. "Minister," he said, "find her a room, a good room. Move someone if you have to; just get it done."

Sands nodded his assent and tried to head for the door as quickly as possible, sensing the awkwardness of the moment. John stopped him and firmly demanded, "I want to greet her upon her arrival at the hotel. No mistakes on this one."

"I understand, sir. Consider it done."

Opening day arrived at the Sovereign Hotel. It was a bright, crisp, sunny day with a slight breeze—perfect.

Previously, John was very aggressive in his push for the opening. Now, he was tentative in light of Carlene's anticipated arrival. Mary had asked if she could skip the opening of the hotel, and he'd readily accepted her wishes. The constant barrage of media, coupled with the tasks associated with the grand opening, weighed heavily upon John, but he was ready.

Sands met John in the opulent lobby of their new creation at nine in the morning. Both men were impeccably dressed in black ties and their finest tuxedoes.

"Minister," John said, "any word from Ms. LeFaze?"

"Not yet," Sands replied, "but she will be here. I've sent a car for her. Just enjoy the opening, sir. This is your day. I'll worry about Ms. LeFaze."

John agreed and made his way to the main doors, ready to greet guests as they crossed the gold-plated threshold. Billionaires, multimillionaires, celebrities, and international elites crowded the main floor. *My, oh my, such beautiful people,* John thought.

The guests were attentive and fawned over the Sovereign, and John was equally appreciative of his guests. In no time, John began to enjoy himself and started to relax despite Carlene's impending presence. After some time, Sands carefully nudged the Sovereign and asked him to start his opening speech. John, acutely aware that Carlene had yet to arrive, attempted to negotiate for additional time, but Sands urged him to begin as the guests grew restless and the press corps from all over the world were in coverage mode.

On a small stage erected in the center of the hotel's lobby, John approached an ornate podium with a large capital "S" affixed to the front. He was flanked by his ministers and several members of his elite Sovereign Guard. As he drew near the microphone, the crowd quieted down, eager for John to begin the festivities.

"Welcome to the Sovereign Hotel, the most elegant hotel in the world," John began.

The crowd applauded briskly.

"Our nation has achieved so many fine accomplishments in less than two years. This hotel, the Sovereign, is reflective of our experience. I welcome you today to our hotel and our country; both are fresh, clean, and beautiful."

John's delivery was smooth, polished, and determined. He paused momentarily to peruse the crowd, and then he saw her. Carlene had arrived dressed unlike any woman in the crowd: radiant, beautiful, and predictably ostentatious. Their eyes met from afar. She smiled, and he gasped briefly before recovering and continuing with the welcome address.

"W-we are so glad that everyone is here today. Let us celebrate together, now and in the future."

Sands, seeming to sense John's sudden change from flawless to mediocre, whispered, "We can wrap up."

Relieved, John told the crowd, "My Minister of Tourism tells me it's time to enjoy and relish the Sovereign Hotel. Thank you."

Carlene moved slowly but steadily toward the podium, the crowd breaking apart so that she could pass easily. John stood motionless as she approached him. Two Sovereign Guards moved toward her as she neared, but John held them back with a gentle wave of his hand. They stood down as John faced his eternal amorous nemesis.

"Carlene, wow, what a nice surprise."

Refusing to take her eyes off of John, Carlene winked at him and whispered, "Oh, really, John? I thought it was you who sent the car for me."

John was rendered defenseless anew and merely stuttered, "Well, I'm surprised and glad they sent the car." He shook her hand. Elated at her presence, the Sovereign inquired meagerly, "Shall we catch up?"

"Sure," Carlene replied. "Tomorrow at nine, coffee?"

"Tomorrow at nine, here at the Sovereign in our Romulus Restaurant."

Hinkins, head of the Sovereign Guard, politely interrupted John as he concluded with Carlene, saying, "Sovereign, we have the British at nine, sir."

"Bump them to ten—no, ten-thirty, General."

"Done, Sovereign. Ten-thirty it is."

Carlene walked off with a wisp of a grin.

For the rest of the day, John wandered around his realm in a euphoric daze. He rehearsed his niceties with guests and was the perfect host. His thoughts, however, were focused on Carlene—Carlene at nine tomorrow morning. He lay awake that night, wondering if his morning rendezvous would be fruitful.

CHAPTER 14

The Sovereign Reigns

The next day, John rose early. Inclement weather had arrived, with a driving rain soaking the nation. John wore a blue suit, blue tie, and his array of self-awarded medals. He arrived at the Sovereign Hotel early and was greeted by the hotel's manager and an entourage of staff.

Carlene arrived about five after nine, untouched by the pouring rain and dressed immaculately in white. Her brunette hair was a striking contrast to her beautiful dress. All eyes were fixed on her as she made her way to John's table in the Romulus Restaurant. The hotel's guests were as captivated by her as their leader.

John shook Carlene's hand, although he yearned for a hug. He pulled a chair out for her, and she sat there, awaiting her coffee.

"Nice place."

"Thanks," John replied. "Sleep well?"

"Yes, very well, but by myself." She giggled.

"Oh, sure, I understand." John looked away as his cheeks grew warm.

Chuckling, she said, "Just teasing, John. It was great. You have a fine place." John was losing the banter of this repartee but felt eager to continue. She spoke again, "So, how is Newland, or whatever you call it?"

The powerful Sovereign would have been offended by anyone else treating his nation so flippantly, but John minded her. "Oh, it's great! Everything is on schedule. I am making history every day. What an adventure."

She looked at him with a stern but sincere gaze and said nothing. Clearly, John was failing to impress her, so he persisted, "I mean, I rule this place the way I want to, the way it ought to be run. If something or someone needs attention, I see to it. No red tape or burrows of bureaucrats; it just gets done."

Carlene nodded. "I see. It's impressive, but what's the end game?" She grinned before adding, "Almighty Sovereign." John took her amusement in stride, watching her every move and savoring her presence despite her testy dialogue.

John finally regained his composure and told her simply, "There is no end." He stirred his coffee. "We are always moving forward and continuing to grow. This is a model state for model people. The world is watching, yearning for what we have."

Suddenly, Carlene blurted out, "How's the wife, John?"

This exclamation stung John. It was the last thing he wanted to talk about with Carlene, but he obliged. "Oh, Mary, yes, she's well. We have a son. It works, Carlene, it works."

"Your marriage sounds just like this place, pragmatic and functional." She lightly teased him, "Moving forward, John?"

Though worn out from her taunts and jabs, John responded with resolve, "I have her full support in everything I do."

"Unlike mine?" Carlene quizzed him.

"No, no. I didn't mean it that way. In fact, you are always welcome here."

She smiled at him and, looking directly into his eyes, said, "I just may visit from time to time."

John was satisfied, though emotionally drained by his lost love. *Or was she?* He'd pined after her for so long that, maybe, he just didn't know how to stop. He wondered if part of him would always be smitten with Carlene.

But Mary, well, there was no doubt that he loved her.

Hinkins appeared with two Sovereign Guards. "The British are here, Sovereign," he said.

Though she was new to the Newland scene, Carlene confidently exclaimed, "Let them drink tea!"

Missing her satire and wanting to be accommodating, John ordered tea for the incoming British dignitaries.

Carlene chuckled, pleased with round one of their reunion, and stood to kiss John on the cheek with a parting, "See you soon."

John watched her stride confidently out of the restaurant. When the British arrived, John was so distracted by his meeting with Carlene that his tea went cold by the time he brought it to his lips for the first sip.

Chapter 15

Newland Advances

Newland's daily progress continued. There were new industries and schools, and tourism flourished. The allure of this ideal state was the international topic du jour. Dignitaries came into Newland in droves from all across the globe. Bright minds, both young and old, applied for citizenship, which was liberally granted to those who met Newland's standards. The Bureau of Citizenry was in full recruitment mode. After the most careful screening process, full citizenship was offered to qualified applicants. It was made abundantly clear that conduct unbecoming a Newland citizen could result in the revocation of Citizen status and further repercussions consistent with Newland law. Undeterred, thousands poured into the nation, and the population boomed. Temporary, or in some cases, probationary status was awarded. Newland needed workers and the best and brightest they received.

John had previously ordered the creation of stock and commodity markets. The investor-friendly tax code made Newland not only a haven for successful, affluent citizens but also attracted capital. Newland's military, which had begun with borrowed equipment from an international donor list, was now listed among the world's top conventional military powers. John, as Sovereign, believed in capitalism and military strength but ordered no incursions or attempts toward a nuclear arsenal. When asked why he had chosen to keep Newland from joining the nuclear club, he said, "Let the nine or ten powers who have incurred the cost to build, maintain, and monitor weapons of mass destruction have that market. Newland is content to maintain a conventional arsenal of state-of-the-art munitions."

John was, however, open to the idea of nuclear power. Given the world's huge reserves of fossil fuels, he pursued the latter in the development of his nation. Just about everything in Newland was controlled by market forces. If it made economic sense or had the potential to do so, it was implemented; if not, John struck it without hesitation.

John carefully played the major military powers against one another. He still readily accepted donations of older planes, ships, and tanks from the United States, Russia, and China. What Newland did not use, they scrapped and recycled. In addition to Newland's military, the Sovereign Guard had grown to ten thousand in number. The Guards were separate from the military but had access to any of the branches, personnel, or resources at the Sovereign's command. As Newland's military presence and might grew, surprisingly, none of its neighbors commented. Some sources placed Newland, despite its small size and population, among the stronger, if not the strongest, conventional fighting force in South America.

Time passed, and Newland eased into its third year. The second anniversary was a holiday but lacked the fanfare of the first event. Prosperity was still the order of the day as Newland continued to succeed. As year three progressed, John summoned his Foreign Minister to his office. All of the original Cabinet officials remained. Napoleon "Nap" Davis was no exception. Davis was bright and well-schooled in the United States and Great Britain. British by birth, Davis was eager to serve. He lamented the fact that his country of birth had let its empire slip away. Though he loved every aspect of British culture, he decried his former nation for its loss of status and power. He eagerly came to Newland to serve its Sovereign and its purpose. John liked Davis and empathized with his Foreign Minister's frustration with his country of origin. John, too, lamented, in his view, America's loss of power and status in the international realm. They sat together in John's office. To get the conversation started, John began with an innocuous, "How are things?"

Davis, ever proper, replied, "Sovereign, Newland is a beacon, a positive force for humanity, a glimpse of the shadow of an ideal state."

"Only a shadow. Why so?" the Sovereign inquired.

Nap, realizing he was professing his ideology to his seemingly infallible leader, responded, "Sovereign, only in the minds of men can the truly ideal state exist, but we can perceive it, visualize it. A nation-state, in my view, can get close, but the human condition—past, present, and future—will keep any nation-state from being perfect. If I may, though, Newland is the best I've ever seen, read about, or envisioned."

John was intrigued, as he was always eager to have a philosophical discussion. However, he knew they needed to move into the realm of the real and practical. "Let's call a conference meeting with our neighbors—those on our direct borders and attached thereto."

Nap replied, "Consider it done, sir. You have my full support, but may I inquire about the purpose of the conference?"

"Sure thing, but consider this classified," the Sovereign said.

Realizing the serious nature of John's demeanor, Nap nodded thoughtfully. "Sovereign," he asked, "please be specific, sir, so that I may follow your orders to the letter."

John realized he had never instilled a "classified" level in Newland. There had never been a need, as he had always ordered what he deemed appropriate, and it was followed.

Accepting this frailty, which he would remedy going forward, John explained, "Nap, for now, my foreign policy for Newland is confidential for only you and me to discuss at this level."

"Yes, sir."

"Later, others will know, but for the present, just us." John had full confidence in Davis for his trustworthy and loyal performance, so he said, "I have assembled an army, air force, and navy. My ships travel up and down two rivers with more pent-up energy than lions trapped in a small cage. I want to have a conference, a meeting with our neighbors. I want Newland to expand."

Davis queried, "Expand, sir?"

"Yes," John said, "grow, Nap, expand our existing borders."

Davis continued his inquiry, "Yes, sir. I think I understand, and I will do whatever you order, but how, sir? How do we expand?"

"That's easy," John said with a wave of his hand. "First, we attempt expansion through diplomacy—your task. If we fail, then militarily—my task."

Davis seemed a bit shaken by the Sovereign's blunt dictates and new goal for Newland, blinking several times in surprise, but he quickly responded with a solid, "Yes, sir."

Pleased with his minister's response, John praised him, "Good. It's settled."

Davis blurted out his fourth or fifth, "Yes, sir," and then inquired anew, "Sovereign, how shall I proceed? How do we persuade them to join us?"

John did not hesitate in his response, "It's Rome revisited. We meet, convene, and invite our neighbors to join us. To become one with Newland. Almost like a United States of South America—under our leadership, of course."

Still reeling from the impact of the Sovereign's desire, Davis carefully posed additional inquiries to his ambitious leader. "May I inquire further, with the utmost respect and unyielding loyalty, sir?"

"Ask away. I am here to assuage you," John replied confidently.

Davis pursued his questions. "What, sir, if the conference is unsuccessful?"

John boomed in a loud and confident voice, "I'll handle that. You set the table; Newland and I shall dine."

Davis shook the Sovereign's hand, left, and copiously prepared the invitations to Newland's neighbors. Davis felt a special glee as he sent good tidings to the surrounding nations. The Sovereign's assurance was enough to remove any second thoughts he might have had. With words of assurance from the Sovereign, the Foreign Minister's concerns withered away.

Chapter 16

The Offer of Kindness

The nations of South America convened according to John's plans and invitations. The communication boldly stated, "An invitation to an offer of kindness." It was so well received that Central American nations asked for invitations to attend. In response to this request, Newland broadened the scope of its outreach and accommodated them.

Only Cuba was not invited, and the Communist loner state did not request an audience. According to Cuba, Newland was viewed as an "offshoot of imperialistic America without the guise of democracy."

This Cuban response did not offend John. He told the press, "The Cubans finally got one right! I am an unabashed capitalist leading a nation of entrepreneurs second to none. Newland will not be deterred by any impediment, be it democratic, bureaucratic, or diplomatic."

John allowed Davis the privilege of opening the conference. The nations all sent their top diplomatic leaders. The international press filled the upper balcony of the Chamber of the People's House in Newland's Sovereignty Building, where they could see the crowded room below, filled with bustling politicians. This group was accustomed to Newland's pomp, circumstance, and never-ending newsworthy status. Today would be no exception.

After Davis's proper and benign address, replete with the niceties and courtesies of the most polished diplomatic corps, John came to the podium at the front of the grand room. John, who wrote his own speeches with the ever-present assistance of his Minister of Information, proceeded atypically, addressing his neighbors in a more bombastic style.

John stated, "Welcome, my friends, to Newland. Many, if not most of you, have been here before, visiting, trading, and witnessing our state from its infancy over two years ago. I wish to stress that all who are here today are present because I deem you friends of Newland, allies to our nation, and partners in our mutual destiny. The inherent greatness in each of you and your countries has been so apparent to me, and I welcome you in that vein."

Despite his loud and pressing tone, the convention erupted in thunderous applause. The bold Sovereign was immediately greeted by a standing ovation, which he was encouraged by. John glanced at the international press corps, once again in awe of the international acclaim the Newland autocrat was receiving.

John continued, "Please, each of you, join us in our quest for greatness. In two and a half years, we have attained things that some civilizations have never accomplished. I will be meeting with every leader here personally to offer you and your nations an alliance of sorts. Consider my overtures to be an offer of kindness, an opportunity to be a part of something the rest of the world will envy and your people will cherish."

The applause erupted again, and John, pleased with his initial foray, concluded his speech. The meetings were set and began. Each nation was allotted fifteen minutes with the Sovereign and his staff to discuss the terms of the offer.

John, who was more conciliatory in the breakout sessions, used every persuasive tool he could muster to gain the support of his neighbors. Davis equally plied his trade and skills, adeptly treating each leader, regardless of their nation's size or power, with overly fawning respect. This special treatment, this artful touch, was directed toward one goal: John wanted his neighbors to be not only an ally of Newland but also a part of Newland.

The presidents and ambassadors listened, pondered, and sorted through their offers. John and his team continued their relentless push to convince them. The first meeting was with Chilean leaders and diplomats. John's offer was concise: "Join us as an ally, a friend, and a partner in commerce, trade, and defense. Newland is ready and able to expand. Chile is a natural partner, a perfect fit."

Chile's ambassador politely but firmly spoke to John while others listened. "Sovereign Kinley, your offer for an alliance with us as articulated is touching and will be considered with the warmth and sincerity in which it has been offered. We must, however, reach out to our citizens, our people. May we get back to you, perhaps, in a month or so?"

Many other leaders responded with the same hesitation. John was frustrated by the hesitant nature of his garnered guests, and he felt the need to move from salesman to political philosopher in his attempt to lure the leaders. He addressed them as a group once more after the individual meetings. "My friends, how many of you are dictators? Please signify by raising your hands." Not a single hand went up. "Exactly!" he exclaimed. "Neither am I. How many of you are strong leaders willing to do whatever is necessary to prevent those in your countries or abroad from harming your people?"

Every hand, including John's, went up.

He continued, "They call me 'Sovereign' in Newland, a title, a name. I call each and every one of you 'Sovereign.'" They all applauded politely. "As Sovereigns, I implore each and every one of you, as leaders, good leaders of your nations, to work with us in Newland. It will benefit your people, the region, and yes, install you in the annuls of history as the great rulers you are."

The Costa Rican president arose and inquired, "Sovereign Kinley, some of us represent democracies. How do you propose we do this without the consent of our people?"

Nodding pensively while he thought out his response, John finally replied, "I dare say, my friend, that if we define democracy, there will be no true democracies in this room." The room grew silent. "I mean no disrespect with my comments, only respect for each of you and for the truth. Search your minds and souls, and then observe your nation. You have been elected or otherwise selected to lead your respective countries. Employ euphemism or whatever 'ism' you deem necessary to govern. Accept this offer of kindness, and your people will reward you with whatever they and you need to bolster your regimes."

The twenty-two leaders began to converse among themselves in hushed voices, pondering Newland's offer. John looked over at Davis, who seemed concerned that there were no immediate takers. He motioned to his Sovereign as if to prod him further. John, keenly aware of what his Foreign Minister was doing, nodded and refocused.

With a nonchalant continuation, John said, "To all our dear friends and neighbors, our offer to join us is, at the present, indefinite. It shall remain open. However, those nations who accept this offer within thirty days will receive an additional fifty million dollars as a token of appreciation from Newland. No constraints, restraints, or dictates as to how the money is to be spent. As Sovereigns in your own reigns, I deem you each worthy to spend the money as you deem fit."

The fifty-million-dollar incentive of kindness clearly attracted the attention of the carefully assembled group. Still, no country accepted or rejected Newland's offer that day, but John and Davis were still undeterred in their quest.

After a grueling day of coaxing his neighbors, John was tired and a bit dismayed. He asked everyone except Nap Davis and Hinkins, the head of his Sovereign Guard, to leave. He then spoke to his two trusted advisors: "Well, gentlemen, what do you think?"

Davis was quick to respond, "Sovereign, I think it's a good start." Davis paused before adding, "At least, there were no 'no's.' There was a lot of interest, and that cash incentive, truly genius, sir."

Hinkins, who was less laudatory of Newland's neighbors, said, "Sovereign, we must press them. They are fools if they reject our offer."

"Understood," John replied.

Ever the diplomat, Davis felt compelled to speak further. "Sovereign, most of these leaders you addressed today are corrupt. Not totally corrupt in a sinister sense, but unlike our Sovereign, who declines pay or self-enrichment for his reign, many of them have profited from their positions. I wonder how much of our eventual generosity will end up in Swiss or Cayman Island accounts to the benefit of their leaders."

John blurted out, "I think you are right, Nap."

Hinkins's head turned abruptly toward his leader.

John continued, "Most leaders, most people, sadly, serve their political party for personal gain. I counted on that when I made my incentivized offer to our guests. Once they buy in, I'll have them, for whatever reason. The cash is a hook of sorts; the real allure is allowing them to do whatever they wish with the funds."

Pleased that his Sovereign was receptive to his train of thought, Davis continued the conversation as the more spartan Hinkins observed in quiet discontent. "Sovereign," Davis inquired, "what will we do if none or few of our neighbors accept your offer?"

John leaned back in his chair and met Hinkins' gaze, who smiled immediately at his leader. John replied, "Gentlemen, for now, we will be patient and optimistic. We shall lead by example, reward any takers, and continue to solicit the others. We have many other tools to employ if necessary. Time is on our side, wealth is on our side, and destiny is on our side."

Hinkins, finally ecstatic, stated, "*You* are on our side."

John had set the table for his fellow leaders for their consideration. His tiny and relatively novice nation was ready to lead a continent. John summoned his Intelligence Minister and ordered him to immediately gather information on the leaders who had attended, their nations, their military and economic strengths, and finally, their political stability. John was steadfast in his belief that the best way to persuade the other nations was through diplomacy, incentives, and peace, though privately, he made decisions regarding other measures should his first line of overtures be ignored.

Chapter 17

Auditing the Ideal State

John was acutely aware that Newland was booming. There was growth everywhere, including an increase in population and profits, and, perhaps most importantly to the Sovereign, Newland's international influence was growing. In his view, John was the power behind the boundless success of Newland, and he was immensely proud of it.

Mary was content as long as John was. John Jr. continued to grow strong, happy, and healthy as Newland's First Child. Honesty ruled the day in Newland, not only with its Sovereign but also with his cabinet members and all who served. To date, only two lower-level bureaucrats have been challenged for alleged dishonest conduct, one in commerce and the other in the Justice Department. After a thorough internal review, they were deemed incompetent rather than dishonest and dismissed. They were, however, able to remain in Newland and pursue other careers, avoiding the ultimate punishment for dishonesty: exile from Newland with no opportunity to return. Incompetence, though not rewarded, was not punished with the severity of the previous vices. John demanded the truth from his Judicial system as well, priding himself that no innocent person had ever been convicted of a crime in Newland. His orders were to use whatever means necessary to extract the truth in any circumstance—civil, criminal, or otherwise.

For the most part, Newland ran efficiently and without pause. The people knew the rules and followed them, and hence, there was little room or desire for disruption. As Sovereign, John had the constitutional power to pardon, exile, or override the Judicial system. To date, he had never seen the need to do so. Petty criminals for theft or minor offenses were severely punished and nationally debased by placing their names and pictures in the news and media, the meticulous details of every mistake published for the public to view. There was little will to be noncompliant in Newland.

Despite the success in Newland, John wanted to know exactly where his "Ideal State" was in terms of wealth and other statistics vital to the country. He summoned his thirteen cabinet ministers and demanded a precise audit from each department head. Not only did John want to know Newland's exact wealth but also the precise sources of revenue. In the absence of income taxes, which John never failed to mention, he wanted to know the percentages of revenue from sales, consumption, and property taxes. He also wanted to know the affluence of Newland's citizens.

Confidently, John ordered a rough draft of this financial information to be delivered to him in thirty days from each cabinet minister. The respective ministers began with an ardent fervor. John had admonished them to present accurate findings with a stern tone bent on absolute truth. He insisted that the results of the audit were to be kept confidential and each minister was to present their facts and figures to the Sovereign alone. Each department head knew John was resolutely serious, as he equated their performance to loyalty to him and to Newland.

Jones, Newland's Minister of Commerce, was concerned. He personally inquired of the Sovereign, "What shall we do, sir, if we encounter difficulties or delays?"

John replied, "Come to me without delay. You will not be punished for honest adversities; just come to see me immediately."

Jones thanked his Sovereign and was pleasantly relaxed with the Sovereign's position. The audit of the "Ideal State" had begun.

At the end of thirty days, a rough draft of compiled data covering close to ten thousand pages was presented to the Sovereign. The document included numbers, statistics, graphs, and analysis. John was impressed but challenged his ministers further. He asked them for summaries: "The data is good, but I want concise numbers so I may make quick decisions."

John was particularly impressed with the military audit, which demonstrated far more strength and depth than previously thought. His second highlight was the well-respected Newland stock and commodity markets, which received international acclaim and investment. The Defense Minister, Jacobs, was particularly relieved. He had overseen the military buildup, which began as a charity venture with a hodgepodge of military hardware from around the world and had become a state-of-the-art conventional fighting force.

Jones and Jacobs were quizzed by the Sovereign about their respective departments. Upon the Sovereign's inquiry, they both opined that Newland's commerce and military, as was borne out by the numbers, were in far better shape than they had projected. John, though stoic, was pleased. He reviewed every department's numbers, and the final summaries were strong.

Newland released its audit numbers to the international press, and the Minister of Information was thrilled. His propaganda was truthful; Newland's numbers were totally verifiable. The Sovereign and the Ideal State were showing the world their formula for national success. In a quote to the state-controlled press, John exclaimed, "This is a political theorem and not political theory."

CHAPTER 18

The Reemergence
of the Three Wise Men

The offer of kindness was neither accepted nor rejected by any of the offerees within the thirty-day deadline. John was surprised but undaunted, and he called Nap Davis and instructed him to keep up all diplomatic pressures and overtures to their neighboring states. John further instructed Davis to keep the incentive money in place for any takers. He wanted to keep all appearances and dialogue positive. With every sector booming, Newland was proud, strong, and growing. Al Grudger had profited from every sector and every transaction as well. He was a broker, an agent, and now, a billionaire. Construction, tourism, infrastructure, military, education, and health care were all strong and expanding.

The population of Newland was approaching two million, and thousands of hopeful, talented people were still streaming in. As Sovereign, John declared himself the first citizen of Newland, but he never renounced his American citizenship or law license. John's Foreign Office had negotiated with the United States for Newland's citizens to be able to hold dual citizenship. Mary and his son held dual citizenship in the States as well, but as John Jr. was born in Newland, unlike his parents, he had birthright citizenship there.

Despite John's most generous offer to Israel and all Jews worldwide, Newland had only received a few hundred requests for joint citizenship. Newland's foreign policy was avowedly pro-Israel. Trade between the two nations was robust and mutually beneficial. John glorified Christianity, especially Roman Catholicism in Newland, but Judaism was honored and protected. The Vatican, despite John's love for the Church and his dogmatic Catholicism, had yet to authorize the construction of a church in Newland. John agreed to be patient. For the present, his evangelical Christian friends filled the churches of Newland.

From foreign policy to franchising his favorite Crumley Cola in Newland, John was still a fan of America in every way. However, he was still kept at a distance by certain American politicians and the press. Dubbed "The American Dictator" by some in the foreign press corps, Americans were generally wary of the Sovereign. The United States had openly opposed the Newland Offer of Kindness. America did, however, trade openly with Newland with no tariffs on either side. John's solace was in economics with his beloved America. In a letter to his finance minister, he wrote, "Trade heals all wounds."

After witnessing Newland's success, Russia and China actively sought trade deals and technology transfers with Newland. John did not trust the Russian Federation, but since they were no longer communist, he traded with them. He cautioned the Russians about spying in Newland. He told their ambassador, "I have no spies in Russia. I expect the same courtesy from you."

The ambassador regarded John, saying, "You value the truth. Russia values survival. If I told you there were no spies in Newland, I'd be a liar."

John, though not pleased with the Russian's response, took comfort that at least he did not lie. John ordered his Intelligence and Security Minister, Burnakov, a former Russian citizen, to have all Russian nationals in Newland watched and followed. Burnakov surprised the Sovereign; he had already done so since his appointment to his post.

China was another topic altogether. Communist in name, capitalist in goal, control, and imperialism, John feared China in every aspect of their relationship. In a letter to his Foreign Minister, he wrote, "The backward Maoist Agrarian China is now the controlled, focused imperial giant of our century. They must be watched, checked, and countered whenever possible."

Al Grudger made his way to his weekly meeting with John in the Sovereignty Building. Everyone knew Al, the American broker, the dealmaker, the man reputed to be the richest man in Newland. Many in Newland's Congress expressed concerns about Al's incredible and insurmountable wealth. Many of John's closest allies in Newland confided in John that Al's wealth was enormous and that they felt it should belong to John. John refused any such offers or initiatives. He prided himself on being the incorruptible Sovereign. In his eyes, a leader should not profit from his or her position. It was unthinkable, a treason of sorts. John was committed to never allowing personal gain from his position to tarnish his reign and the reputation of his beloved Newland.

Al arrived in the finest fashion. Immaculately groomed, he glowed as he entered John's office. John could not help but think he was the visual antithesis of his father, Sam, who, despite his wealth, never lost the ruffled plebian look of tattered attire. Al entered and said, "Morning, John. Doing well?"

John replied with his usual, "Yes, great. Forward, always moving forward." John was especially happy that day, having learned that Mary was expecting again. "Bet you love being a citizen of Newland—no income taxes!"

Al, equally as buoyant, replied, "I am, but I am filling Newland's coffers to overflowing with that odious sales tax. Every time I buy something paltry or palatial, I get tapped."

"Al," John said, "You always make my day when you lament consumptive taxes. They are the fairest collectible revenue source for a nation. Think about it, Al. The poor, of which we have so few in Newland, pay it, our middle class pay it, and the wealthy pay it based on choices—from necessities to luxuries. It's taxation's closest allegiance to the truth."

Al had learned early in his role as profiteer of Newland never to debate or question John about policy. He merely smiled and told John, "Next time I buy one of those Crumley Colas, I'll think of you. From Sovereign to serf, all pay the same."

John was elated anytime tax policy was discussed. He had always railed against wealth redistribution under the guise of what his critics called "progressive."

"Progressive," he once wrote, "is allowing an individual, business, or any productive entity to retain its resources to the fullest extent possible." John was especially enjoying his visit with Al that day. He spoke further, "Know what's great about Newland, Al?"

"Everything," the mercenary said in the most attentive manner.

"Good answer," the Sovereign replied. "Its business," he extolled. "Its business and businesspeople. Men and women who understand and live in a real world, a world true to markets.

Businesspeople are problem solvers. Markets don't lie, and they can't be lied to indefinitely. Eventually, they correct themselves and their economies, often to the detriment of pandering states that ignored or hid the truth from their people."

The Sovereign was preaching to Al, who was agnostic about ideology and prophetic only for profit. In any event, he minded the Sovereign and the Sovereign minded him. John, finally realizing his rhetoric was redundant, decided to cease his "sermon on the count."

Taking advantage of John's pause from his lecture, Al grew serious. "John," he said, leaning forward. "I came by today on a serious note."

John replied, "Sure thing, Al. You have listened to me for hours on end. Glad to hear from you—any topic you choose."

Al began, "Do you remember those three men Sam introduced you to years ago at the law office?"

A bit taken aback by Al's recounting, John replied, "Sure, I remember them. I hadn't thought about them for years, though. They came, they offered, and I conquered." John chuckled awkwardly so as not to seem too concerned.

Al hesitantly replied, "They want to meet with you."

John remained still for over a minute. He thought deeply, carefully pondering his decision. Finally, after a slight grimace, he told Al, "Sure, I'll meet with them." It was obvious to John that Al, like his father before him, was CBA's messenger. He quizzed Al about the meeting. "What do they want? And why now?"

Al looked directly at Newland's leader but could only offer minimal assistance. He told John, "Maybe they will tell you. Maybe we will finally know. I'll set up a meeting."

John agreed. "Do it here, my office, Al," John insisted.

"Got it," Al replied.

Still bewildered by the request, John continued, "This is odd, very odd. I wish I knew why and who they were." Rattled, John asked Al, "Perhaps Sam could join us?"

Al quickly responded, "Oh, they don't even want me in the meeting, just you and them." There would be no pomp, cameras, or fanfare, just CBA and the lone Sovereign.

The disarmed leader pressed on, "You mean no aides, assistants, no help whatsoever?"

"That's it, John. That's the way it was presented to me."

John stood erect and directed Al, "Set the meeting. I'll be there. I'll handle everything."

Al nodded, patted John on the shoulder with an understanding touch, and departed.

CHAPTER 19

Three on One

John had Al set the meeting early, seven o'clock, for breakfast. John was decidedly sharper in the morning. He had stayed awake the night before, wondering about the meeting to come. That morning, he gave Mary and John Jr. a parting kiss and was driven to the Sovereignty Building by two of his Sovereign Guards. By all appearances, this seemed like a typical day for John, except for the impending meeting.

John arrived early, pensive. His aides greeted him in his office. They inquired about the office setup and asked if they could assist their leader in any way. John was solely focused on the upcoming meeting. He expressed his pleasure with the office and sat in his chair, awaiting the arrival of his guests.

"Please, leave me now," he told his aides.

Somewhat perplexed, they inquired further about his guests and the breakfast.

John realized that he must have seemed thankless as the array of breakfast foods and their corresponding aromas engulfed the room. "This is private today. Please show my guests in when they arrive. Thank you."

General Hinkins's top aide and an able colonel seeking a star from his Sovereign, Kinder, observed the stern uneasiness in his leader. Kinder was a fixture in this office as much as John was, being one of his personal guards. He knew better than to interfere in his Sovereign's affairs, but today, Kinder could tell something was off. "Sovereign, call me if you need anything. Anything at all."

John said, "Thank you. You have done well. I have a lot on my mind. You may go now."

Kinder nodded his understanding and left.

John sat in his office, consumed by a sense of loneliness and impending dread. The very nature of the vague and indirect motives, desires, and direction of the CBA investors left John pining for details, explanations, and clarity.

At seven o'clock sharp, the trio of Combs, Burns, and Amos arrived. They were dressed exactly as John remembered, handsomely groomed and eerily alike.

They entered the room, and John greeted them. "Good morning, gentlemen."

He shook all three's hands, and Combs, in the most unemotional tone, replied, "Good morning, John. So good to see you."

This was the most positive comment he had ever extracted from the CBA. John was mildly encouraged. He smiled—they did not. Combs continued, "I am sure you remember Burns and Amos?"

"Yes, of course. Great to see all of you," John replied.

John offered his visitors a sumptuous breakfast.

"Coffee, just coffee, will do," Combs said, brushing off the rest of John's offer. John was eagerly attentive to his three guests. He poured coffee for all, and they sat.

John desperately wanted to move the conversation forward, so he said, "Gentlemen, Al indicated that you wanted to meet."

Combs, the exclusive spokesman of the trio, leaned forward and, in his ever-present monotone, responded, "CBA, on behalf of its investors, wanted to meet." He sipped his coffee robotically and continued, "For almost three years now, the venture has continued without supervision, intervention, or otherwise. A trillion dollars of capital in addition to millions in incidentals was raised, advanced in order to finance this deal."

John had been silent to this point, listening intently, but finally felt compelled to comment. "Deal? What exactly do you mean, Combs?"

In an uncanny unison, Burns and Amos raised their heads.

John continued, "I have founded a state, a nation. We have prospered, grown, and succeeded. I can share the books with you."

All three of his guests were momentarily silent. John felt a need to prove his point further, to prove his success in this so-called "deal."

"These are not 'cooked books.' It's all truthful: every statistic, every number, every fact. I have accomplished what Caesars could not." John was now leaning forward, reminiscent of his trial lawyer days, studying and convincing his three triers of fact.

Seemingly unaffected, Combs continued, "No need to look at the books. We read newspapers, watch television, and study markets. Newland is what it is."

John was irked by Combs' stoic irreverence to his ideal state and pushed back. "Look, Combs, gentlemen, I'll be direct. I, we, have attained the unattainable. Here in Newland, we are the envy of the world. Growth, success, and prosperity are everywhere. We are a safe nation, efficient and honest. Surely, you have noticed."

Combs, focusing on the CBA agenda, ignored the Sovereign's boasts and replied, "Our concern is only our investors' return on their investment."

John, perhaps still more irked than puzzled, addressed his de facto board of directors. "Gentlemen, I don't understand. Who are you? You return after three years and nebulously demand a return on investment. I've given my life for this place and done it well." The Sovereign's confidence returned as he faced the CBA team. He regained his momentum and pressed them, "I want answers. No, I demand answers."

Combs and his partners were unmoved by John's outcry.

Combs told him, "We provided you the means to play your games as they were. You have enjoyed three years of unabated freedom."

John interrupted, "The deal was, Combs, as I recall, that I would possess free reign to build a nation, no strings attached."

Combs merely leered at Newland's founder and berated him in an unimpressed tone. "Come on, John, no strings attached? Really?" he said bluntly. "It's not important who we are or who we represent. To us, you are no Sovereign. We deem you a pawn, a mere pawn. Just sit back and listen."

John was struck by the demeaning lecture from Combs and decided to hear him out. In bewildered amazement, he sat back and listened.

Combs continued, "Why do you think that none of your neighbors accepted your 'offer of kindness'?" John did not reply. Burns and Amos showed emotion for the first time; sinister grins spread on each of their faces as Combs pummeled the isolated Sovereign. "Why do you think Newland has done so well on paper?"

John could not remain silent. "Paper?" he exclaimed. "Newland is more than facts and figures on paper; it's a state, a nation, a powerful country. We do what other nations dream of doing: success after success. So, do I get answers, at least some modest praise?"

Combs replied, "You received a visit. A chance to meet with your investors."

For the first time ever with the CBA group, John became sarcastic. "Gee, thanks. You really know how to thank a visionary."

"We are not interested in visions or visionaries. You are lucky enough to receive a visit."

Heated, John demanded, "What do you want? A check? Stock? Make me an offer."

"We already have," Combs responded.

John looked over at Burns and Amos and exclaimed, "You two, the silent ones, what do you want?"

Burns smiled cautiously, and in a Scottish brogue, he tersely exclaimed, "Lad, Combs speaks for us."

Without prodding, Amos added, "Sí, Señor. Combs speaks for us."

Growing tired of the conversation, Combs renewed his blunt response to John, saying, "We are who we are; we represent who we represent. If you want your trains to run, planes to fly, banks to bank, you will comply."

By this time, John was numb in disbelief. He replied with all of his emotion to the CBA. "I cannot believe your group.

You have witnessed the formation and success of an ideal state. It works. Surely, you want to be a part of this."

Combs, Burns, and Amos were unmoved and sat motionless. Finally, Combs spoke, "It's time for us to go now. We will be in touch."

John persisted, still dissatisfied by the results of the meeting, "Gentlemen, please, I will not yield to a solemn goodbye. I am at a loss to address your concerns or, for that matter, mine. I implore you to stay and speak more, explain more, negotiate more."

The CBA trio stood up in the most aloof manner and began to depart.

John continued, "I'll put you up at the Sovereign Hotel or the Verdad if you prefer. You still befuddle me. Do not belittle me! Stay in Newland and communicate."

As Combs, Burns, and Amos continued to try to escape the meeting, John followed them, peppering them with questions and comments. He shouted, "Are you allies? Foes? Please stop this game of nebulous diplomacy."

Combs replied in his parochial fashion, "We will be in touch. Directly or indirectly, but John, we are certainly not diplomats."

John finally retorted, "We can finally agree on one thing: you are not diplomats."

Combs, Burns, and Amos exited. John sat down at his desk alone in his office, rattled by the rancorous standoff that had just ensued. The scent of aging breakfast dominated the room, overwhelmingly the dismay that preyed upon his mind. After an hour alone, John arose from his chair and left his office to return home to Mary and John Jr. for the remainder of the day.

CHAPTER 20

The Road to Nowhere

John lay awake another night. Tossing and turning, thinking back on the words of the CBA. He was unsure of how to proceed. For almost three years, his word as Sovereign had been law. His orders and ideas sprang into action without delay. For the first time in a long time, John felt a blend of hesitation and confusion; these feelings were as unwelcome to him as they were foreign. Rarely did he discuss issues of state with Mary. On occasion, he discussed and implemented educational policies to her liking based on her past experience, success, and passion for the subject. These policies all proved to be successful and beneficial, especially at the elementary school level. Most of the time, Mary showed up, supported her husband, and doted on John Jr. This morning was different. Mary sensed her omnipotent husband was at a complete loss.

John looked over at Mary as the morning light entered their bedroom. Mary lovingly gazed at her husband, who was clearly in distress. He was atypically silent, so she spoke, "Care to talk about it?"

John murmured in a quiet, defeated tone, "Yes."

She responded softly but clearly, "Good. Let's chat."

John remained silent for a while, then finally said, "Mary, I was paid a visit. An interesting but odd visit."

Mary prodded him to continue; he did. "Three men came to see me—three of the strangest men I have ever met."

"Clearly, they have upset you. I rarely see you so ill at ease, so unnerved."

John agreed.

Mary inquired further, "What did they say?"

John sighed, then explained warily, "It's what they didn't say. They wouldn't commit to anything and wouldn't tell me what they wanted. I met them years ago with Sam Grudger. They made me the offer to build this place, and I did it—I built a nation. Not only did I build it, but I built it right. Now, they have shown up, and well, who knows?"

Mary thought and then responded, "Is Al involved?"

"Not exactly." He then corrected himself, "Only as a conduit."

"Did they make any specific demands? Requests?"

John responded, shaking his head in a quandary, "I am not sure."

Mary sensed the magnitude of this situation and inquired further, "John, are you, are we, in danger?"

John candidly responded, "I don't think so. The visit was more like a group of investors checking on their investment, but they know we are booming. If it's money they wanted, they would have demanded a figure. An amount, an offer, a deal. They did none of the above."

Mary thought deeply for a while and then offered a solution. "Assemble your most loyal supporters, call a meeting, and come up with a plan to combat this. I will help you." She continued as adamantly as he had ever known Mary to be, "John, loyalty to you is most crucial. You must confront the situation with these three. Collect facts, ask questions, get answers, and then take action. Use your best judgment. Who would stand with you if you were the last man standing in Newland?" Looking into his eyes, she reiterated, "I want unfettered, resolute, unshakable people around you to deter and defeat this threat."

Impressed with Mary's resolve, John said, "That's it!"

Mary went on, "You need a legion of loyalists to help you."

John began to think aloud, "My Sovereign Guard."

"Yes," Mary said, "that's a start. They are loyal but not smart, I mean, not smart in a savvy way."

John agreed.

"How about your Cabinet? They are loyal and very adept," Mary suggested.

He further agreed. "Brilliant minds, most of them. I agree." The ideological leader could not help himself but profess a bit. "Mary," he said. "Most people have an affinity for winners and an aversion toward losers."

Mary, who was rarely critical of her vociferous husband, retorted, "John, your reign is threatened; get your head out of the clouds. This is no time to play philosopher king. Newland needs a pragmatic leader."

Stunned by her rebuke, John paused and ceased his lecture. Mary was again in control of the situation and continued, "Choose two or three in your Cabinet to assist you. Surely, you must have some favorites."

John groped for a solution and suggested Al Grudger.

Mary lamented his choice. "Choose a mercenary and expect mercenary results. Al will assist if it benefits Al and will bail if it suits his needs. He may already be on their team for all we know. Self-interest will suit him. Use him as he uses you. Never trust him unless you are positive his needs are at stake in your crisis."

Though lingering in despair, John was impressed with Mary's advice and decided to heed it and follow her dictates. Though impressed with her wisdom under pressure, he failed to convey his compliments or thanks. He merely nodded, gazing at her, and said, "Done. I'll do it."

The next day, John hurriedly convened a meeting in his office. He did not invite Al Grudger but chose Hinkins, head of his Sovereign Guard; Glitz, head of his Ministry of Information; Parmano, Minister of Commerce and Trade; and Davis, Minister of Foreign Affairs. In his view, he had military might, propaganda, trade, and diplomacy as his ingredients to address the diet of Combs, Burns, and Amos.

Doors were closed with the strictest instructions for no interruptions. John and his chosen four Newlanders were about to embark on a plan for survival. They convened, ate, drank, and copiously studied the baffling predicament of the Ideal State. John, honest and transparent to the core, laid out the entire situation for his advisors. At the conclusion of the explanation of Newland's situation, John opened the floor for suggestions. Hinkins abruptly offered to have the CBA trio assassinated, personally handled by him, if the Sovereign so ordered. This course of action was unanimously dismissed by all the others, including John, as they quickly asserted that Combs, Burns, and Amos were probably just agents or fronts for a much larger group. Glitz suggested an informational campaign aimed at discrediting the trio through Newland's extensive communications network. This idea was also summarily dismissed by the others as too vague in light of the magnitude of the CBA threat.

Before they adjourned, the ad hoc committee finally agreed on some basic tenets. First, they agreed that Newland needed to continue on its current paths in all directions. The nation-state had been successful to date, and the group wanted the good fortune to continue. Second, they decided not to alarm the populace of Newland until it became absolutely necessary for the survival of the State. John knew he had gambled on confiding in his ministers about the CBA and their history. They were sworn to silence, all agreeing the fewer persons aware of the situation, the better. Third, they agreed that the select group of five would meet weekly to discuss the situation until the danger that CBA presented to Newland had passed or was abated. Finally, they agreed that John should employ whatever resources were necessary to quantify the CBA menace and to discover more specific facts about the matter. The group understood this enemy was less transparent, less visible, and less direct than most foes.

Though utterly exhausted, John thanked each of his ministers before departing. The Sovereign was in a struggle with an amorphous enemy he had never imagined. He was committed to fighting this illusive foe with total resolve.

John continued his quest to disarm the CBA threat by ordering all of Newland's intelligence resources to investigate the threat. Burnakov, his Head of Intelligence, convinced John to keep surveillance methods in place on Newland's neighbors and its own people. John was acutely aware that the Ministry of

Intelligence regularly monitored its citizens at will. However, after meeting with Burnakov, he was surprised at the depth of the surveillance and who was tracked by the Russian immigrant. John readily agreed to Burnakov's requests.

For the next several weeks, nothing of new significance happened on the intelligence front. No further contacts from the CBA. Newland continued to prosper, and perhaps most importantly, Newland's intelligence ministry was unable to obtain any information about the CBA, its members, its purpose, or the like. Newland spent millions of dollars on this quest, and its best assets were deployed domestically and internationally, yet the CBA's existence was as mysterious as it was from its inception. John summoned Burnakov to his office for a one-on-one meeting to discuss this dilemma.

John, though frustrated with the lack of progress toward the CBA investigation, knew his Intelligence and Security Ministry was strong and flexible. Burnakov had given Newland an internal and external intelligence presence, and despite the lack of information about the CBA, the agency was formidable. Burnakov had proven his loyalty to John in the way he ran the intelligence operations. For instance, minor critiques of the Newland regime were tolerated from within its borders, but not-so-subtle visits from The Agency usually quelled the dissenting voices. If criticisms persisted beyond the pale of what John or the Ministry felt acceptable, action was taken. A few exiles had occurred, but most Newlanders acquiesced and were silent.

Despite the Ministry's general success, the CBA remained an anathema. John personally sat with Burnakov for hours, reviewing records, summaries, and films. Nothing was forthcoming. After months of frustration, John exclaimed to his

Head of Intelligence, "What is this noxious group of affluent meddlers?"

In a defeated tone, Burnakov merely replied, "I just don't know. I'm still working on it. I will find out, Sovereign. This is my quest. I apologize for the delay, but I will see this mission to its conclusion."

John thanked him and dismissed him to continue his search.

CHAPTER 21

The Reemergence of Carlene

Newland roared into its fourth year as a continuing success. The Sovereign Hotel booked out months in advance, as did its sister hotel, La Verdad. Tourism boomed as travelers came to the Ideal State in pilgrimage fashion. Many tourists, swayed by the wondrous allure of Newland, decided to apply for citizenship status. Despite the CBA's inquiry over a year earlier with no resolve or further comment, John was satisfied with his beloved Newland.

Mary and John had their second child, another son, whom they named Sam. They were happy. Mary adored John, not as the Sovereign of a modern-day empire, but as her John, the struggling young lawyer whom she loved long ago. Her love for him was unabated, as was his for her. John loved Mary for her love, loyalty, and kindness. His affection for her was deep and comfortable. She was his friend and confidant, but most importantly, his emotional backstop. Regardless of the issue of the day, Mary was always there to support her beloved John.

Despite their enduring and strong relationship, John's thoughts often wandered toward Carlene. He was kept abreast of her comings and goings at the Sovereign Hotel, which were quite frequent. She steadfastly refused to stay at La Verdad. Carlene had become a favorite at the local gatherings and a guest in demand at social events for the Newland elite. She maintained her American citizenship despite pleas from her new friends to join them as a Newlander. On occasion, John would run into her at parties. He was still smitten by her beauty and her uncanny ability to render him awkward.

The Deemers were among Newland's most prominent citizens. Originally British, they brought their billions to Newland in the country's very first year. The tax structure was alluring to the patriarch, Mark Deemer, and his wife, Elizabeth, and they gladly traded their United Kingdom brand for that of Newland. At their first party, Elizabeth had boldly proclaimed, "I was once a British citizen. We were once an empire, a colonial giant. I left a nation of mediocrity and malaise for an empire of promise."

Mark agreed with her sentiments, and they were among Newland's proudest citizens. The Deemers threw lavish parties, replete with international visitors and local guests. John, their beloved Sovereign, was a regular guest at such events. The tee-totaling ruler enjoyed the festivities and interaction with the crowds. John, in fact, made it a point to visit several parties throughout the year. He was always welcomed with open arms.

John was perusing his invitations for the week and noticed that Carlene had submitted an RSVP for the Deemers' upcoming bash. Mrs. Deemer and John had become close friends. John admired her polished and elegant style and genuine friendship. Although a bit portly, she was radiant and instantly gained John's approval. Over the years, their friendship and mutual admiration had flourished. John felt at ease when he visited the Deemers.

John had maintained that, despite standard English as the official language of Newland, his nation or any great nation must add new words of sufficient value to the vernacular.

To honor Elizabeth, John tasked her with the duty of adding new English words to the official dictionary of Newland. She was an aficionado of languages, especially English, and gladly accepted his directive. Mrs. Deemer's first addition to Newland's dictionary was the term "Sovereignjohn." The term was defined in two ways. First, as a noun, was "an absolute leader with immense powers over a nation-state." The verb definition was even more interesting, gaining the meaning of "the act of problem-solving in a quick, efficient, and successful manner." In total, over one hundred words were added to Newland's official English dictionary by Elizabeth Deemer.

Saturday night arrived, the night of the Deemer's upcoming party. The weather was perfect, and a warm setting sun set the Deemer mansion aglow as the guests arrived. Security was always abundant at Newland parties with a mix of private security, state police, and the usual smattering of obsequious Sovereign Guards. John arrived early, at seven o'clock sharp. Flanked by four Sovereign Guards, he was one of the first guests to arrive. He wore his best tuxedo in lieu of his official uniform. By design, he longed to see Carlene. The Deemers greeted John joyfully as Mark Deemer exclaimed, "The Sovereign has arrived!"

Soon after, guests streamed into the residence, with the overflow of visitors entering a huge yard adorned with statues and gardens. This was John's crowd; he was jubilant. Wealthy people and wealthy guests, and he was their idol.

John smiled broadly and greeted every guest. He was eagerly awaiting Carlene's arrival. Every time the door opened, allowing new guests to enter the opulent mansion, John peered in that direction, hoping it was his longtime female challenge. He remained witty and cordial as the guest attendance mounted, but he was solely focused on one guest.

Carlene arrived at eight o'clock, impeccably dressed and stunning. John, somewhat emotionally attenuated by her delayed arrival, eyed her entrance into the room. He experienced an odd fatigue as he walked toward the doorway. The Deemers greeted Carlene with the usual enthusiasm afforded their visitors. They relished the opportunity to add new members to their ranks as cherished guests, especially powerful, connected persons. Like most Newlanders, they knew John had a long-standing relationship with the radiant brunette and gleefully accepted her presence.

John approached the Deemers from behind and glanced at Carlene. She smiled widely at him, which pleased him. The Deemers parted as John greeted Carlene with his typical sheepish "good to see you" greeting.

Carlene playfully quizzed him. "So, how is the Sovereign?"

John merely said, "Fine as usual." John's attention was focused on Carlene, which was apparent to the throngs of guests who watched the two converse.

Looking around, Carlene teased, "Sovereign of the Doorway, maybe we should sit and talk?"

"Uh, sure," John agreed sheepishly.

A server appeared at their small table, assigned by the Deemers to ensure their Sovereign wanted for nothing in their domain. John ordered champagne for Carlene and sweet tea for himself. The two sat and talked, oblivious to the guests who strolled by. Caviar and salmon with a host of other delicacies arrived at the table. They dined and chatted.

As midnight approached, guests began to depart. Carlene, noting the late hour, said, "John, oh my, it's late. I guess we should depart." John reluctantly agreed, awash with disappointment at the waning of time.

As they walked toward the door, John, feeling especially confident, commented, "Carlene, why don't we meet more often?"

Carlene, ever the opportunist, nodded in agreement but teasingly said, "But whatever will we talk about?"

John, deaf to her ribbing, firmly said, "On the first of every month, nine a.m. in my office. What a way to start each month." After a brief pause, he continued, "By the way, next week is the first."

Carlene smiled. "I'll be there." With those words, she patted him gently on the shoulder. As she departed, she dropped her voice low, saying, "There will be no hugs or kisses for you tonight." She laughed as she walked down the front steps.

Still pining for her presence, John paused and awkwardly called after her, "Need a ride somewhere?"

"I'm good, John," she said. "I stay at the Sovereign. Great place, you know. I have a room there, pretty permanent. Demand is high, though, sure hope I can keep it."

"Call me if you have any problems," John insisted. She grinned and exited as the Sovereign looked longingly after her.

Chapter 22

The Status Quo

In its fifth year of existence, Newland continued to experience exponential growth in all sectors. John's monthly meetings with Carlene earned her great wealth as she lobbied him on behalf of various interest groups. She was no Al Grudger, who continued on his path to billions, but she did well. John was more than glad to accommodate her. He knew she was profiting from her access to him, but he adored the time they spent together.

As Newland expanded, Al continued as "Broker in Chief." He built the largest mansion in Newland as a testament to his ever-increasing prosperity. Al met regularly with John, updating him on Newland's opportunities. John's only recurring frustration was Al's inability, or so it seemed, to provide answers on the CBA situation. The CBA still lay dormant, but they were ever-present in John's mind. The Sovereign pressed Al in every meeting for information, contacts, or any sign of communication. Al's response was always consistent: "None, John, none."

The collective wealth of Newland was still growing, as was its population. Through careful city planning and facilities design, new citizens easily integrated into the small nation. Every aspect of Newland society was efficient and orderly as miscues were promptly addressed, resolved, and settled. John, though confident and bold, was still amazed at the success of

Newland. He was, however, still puzzled that no country had accepted Newland's Offer of Kindness. The neighboring countries in the region were in economic turmoil but rejected an amicable joining with John's ideal state.

A large island off the coast of South America had recently declared its independence with the blessings of its former colonial power. Newland was landlocked in South America, but the new nation, Imploria, was an island roughly the size of Newland, with a population of eight hundred thousand. It was a tourist hub with a largely agrarian economy.

One year after independence, the fledgling nation was struggling but proud, with only a skeletal military and domestic police force in place. John had longed to be rid of the landlocked nature of Newland. He wanted access to the sea to facilitate commerce and expansion. These goals made Imploria an ideal target for the Ideal State. Chile had refused Newland a permanent right of way purchase to the sea. This nation, unlike Imploria, had too formidable of a military to risk a conflict. John increasingly feared an alliance of Newland's neighbors against him. Imploria provided a solution to that threat.

John convened his entire Cabinet in a closed session. There was none of the usual pomp and circumstance; this was just a classified meeting of Newland's leadership. John rose and assured his ministers that the meeting would be brief and concise. John explained his desire to add Imploria to Newland's realm, not as an ally, but as a new territory. The Cabinet was silent as John explained his reasons for this desired acquisition. Once he finished his explanation, John asked the attendees if they had any questions. Hinkins, head of the Sovereign Guard, spoke, "Sovereign, will Imploria be part and parcel of Newland or a colony, sir?"

John promptly responded, "Imploria will not be a colony. The expansion of Newland means that all citizens of Imploria must become Newlanders. This will be a state of sorts."

John looked across the silent, sullen room. He inquired, "Any objections?" There was silence. "Very well, Ministers, I shall lay out the plan for the expansion of Newland." John stood and articulated his plan, "I will dispatch our Foreign Minister, Davis, to meet with President Hernando of Imploria."

Hernando was a popular leader in Imploria who had been a longtime advocate for independence from hundreds of years of colonial domination. The offer was simple. Thirty days for Imploria to join as part of Newland. Hernando would remain as the leader of Newland's new state, with all citizens, including Hernando, possessing the rights and privileges of Newland's citizens. English would replace Spanish as the official language, but Spanish could be legally spoken. The entire thrust of the offer to Hernando was to stress Newland's desire to make Implorians into Newlanders. A peaceful, seamless absorption of Imploria by Newland.

Nap Davis, the Foreign Minister, offered to draft a letter of introduction the next day. Without saying a word, John reached into his pocket and produced a letter. "It's done and ready. Travel there and deliver it tomorrow," he said, holding the letter out to Davis.

Davis agreed to depart immediately for Imploria. "Sovereign, what shall I do if I am rebuffed?"

John responded, "Return to me immediately with Hernando's response, regardless of his decision."

"Understood, sir. I shall."

John stood erect as his Ministers watched, in awe of this bold move. He addressed them confidently, saying, "This will begin a new era in Newland's history—an expansion of our greatness, our values, our very being. We must succeed with Imploria and beyond. Let us resolve to bring Imploria into Newland with relative ease." Then, John dismissed his Cabinet.

As they departed, he stopped the head of his Sovereign Guard. "Hinkins," he said, "Please remain. I must confer with you about our military."

The two men spoke for four hours longer. Finally exhausted, they parted.

Chapter 23

To Implore Imploria

Davis, the Foreign Minister, arrived in Imploria early the next day. He appeared unannounced at the capitol building and asked to see President Hernando. Davis was greeted by several friendly bureaucrats. He had visited Imploria several times, both before and after its independence. It helped that Davis was known not only in Imploria but also internationally as an honest and gifted diplomat.

Upon learning of Davis' arrival, Hernando promptly summoned him to his office. The office, which smelt of cigar smoke, matched the rugged but strong appearance of the young diplomat. Hernando greeted the Foreign Minister with a glowing smile that wrinkled the corners of his dark eyes. "So, how is the Sovereign?"

Davis felt a bit uneasy about the task ahead of him and his current circumstances, so he answered sheepishly, "Well, Mr. President, very well, thanks. He sends his best." An awkward malaise gripped him as he pondered his next words. He finally added, "I am so glad you call him Sovereign, Mr. President, especially in light of what I am about to discuss with you."

Hernando, still smiling and offering pleasantries, replied, "Minister Davis, you are a friend, and so is your Sovereign.

Newland, your beloved country, is clearly an ally of Imploria. Please speak up. Surely you don't bring unpleasant news from Newland?"

Davis, now struggling to phrase his words, could only muster, "No, no, not at all, Mr. President. In fact, I have a very special letter for you from the Sovereign."

He presented the letter to Hernando and remained silent.

Hernando chuckled before opening the letter and quipped, "Perhaps another offer of kindness?" This comment caused Davis to freeze as the unknowing leader of Imploria was about to be showered with "kindness" in the form of a much more potent offer.

As Hernando opened the envelope, Davis felt compelled to speak, "Mr. President, I am a messenger, solely a messenger."

Hernando grew more serious in appearance, reading the letter as perspiration poured down both sides of Davis' face. Hernando, now devoid of a smile, grew sullen and serious. He raised his head and looked directly at the Sovereign's emissary, his face aching with displeasure.

He spoke to Davis sternly and with an uncanny directness usually not found in the dialect of diplomacy. "Minister, I will be straightforward. I have lived my entire life dedicated to Imploria's independence. For hundreds of years, our beautiful island was a colony, a mere pawn of Miruba, Imploria's mother country. We are finally free—free and independent. I concede, poorer, much poorer than before, but free."

Davis hung on every word Hernando articulated in a modest attempt at respect and merely uttered, "I understand."

Hernando continued, "I represent the bastion of the people's request, total independence. I could never agree to these terms." Sensing the uneasiness of Newland's messenger, Hernando spoke further, "Nap, I'm not offended."

Davis looked up, sensing a partial reprieve.

Hernando continued, "I am not. I know John; he's ambitious, bright, and aggressive. I wish he would search elsewhere. Can he and I speak directly?"

Davis, known for his abundant honesty, replied, "I don't know, Mr. President. It's probably best to write him a letter in response. I will deliver it promptly."

Hernando agreed and promptly grabbed a pen from his desk and a piece of paper from a tattered pad and wrote his response.

John,

Call me. I must decline your offer, but please call me. I want to avoid hostilities with a friend, if possible.

Respectfully,
Hernando

Hernando handed the letter to Davis, who shook Hernando's hand and then departed. Davis then flew back to Newland and hand-delivered the response to his Sovereign. Davis was silent as he handed the note to John. John neither praised, criticized, nor questioned Davis. Finally, he quietly dismissed him from his office.

John sat alone in his office, reading and rereading Hernando's response. It was once again decision-making time for Newland's Sovereign.

CHAPTER 24

Hernando

The next day, John called Hernando. The call went through swiftly, and both men eagerly awaited the conversation. John spoke first, "Hernando, it's John."

Hernando sensed the Sovereign's tone and responded, "John, thanks for at least a call. I—"

John interrupted Hernando and said sternly and tersely, "Hernando, I like you. I like Imploria. I prefer peace to war, diplomacy to aggression, and amicability to hostility."

Hernando refused to be stampeded by John's rhetoric and interrupted him, "So do I."

John continued in a polite rant, "Imploria can be part of our ideal state. Surely, you've seen everything we have accomplished. With the stroke of your pen, Imploria goes from poor to rich, menial to important, fearful to feared, and you, Hernando, will be Governor of Imploria, our new state—the crown jewel of Newland!"

Hernando was a wise man; he knew John could have attacked his island nation without notice or concern. On one hand, Hernando appreciated the fact that John was trying to incentivize their merger. Still, he was reluctant. "What am I to do? I thank you profusely for your offer. It's almost Roman in tradition, isn't it?"

John, startled by the president's knowledge, replied, "Impressive, Hernando, very impressive, Roman it is."

John had forgotten that Hernando had been Oxford-educated. He might have started out as an island peasant, but he came back to Imploria well-versed in history and politics and desiring to be free. He taunted John a bit in light of John's play for Imploria, saying, "Thanks, John, but Newland is no Rome, and you, sir, are no Caesar."

Insulted, John replied, "You are right. We are better than Rome."

Surprised by the Sovereign's hubris, Hernando challenged him, "Five years of good fortune, and you dare to take on the centuries and legacy of Rome?"

John stood his ground. "We are the most efficient and impressive nation the world has ever seen. I am proud to represent, exemplify, and promote that."

Hernando responded with vehement disbelief, "No, take it from a peon patriot of an insignificant island nation. You used to represent the greatest empire ever when you served in your other life."

John was bewildered by Hernando's comments and pushed back, "Really, Hernando? I left gridlock, inefficiency, and decadence, a full downward spiral."

Hernando was undeterred. "America is the world's greatest empire. In everything it does, right or wrong, roars or snores, it rivals the planet."

John realized he was not going to convince Hernando of Newland's supremacy, so he regrouped his verbal attack and changed his approach. "Enough about America. We are here; they are there."

Hernando held firm, "Where do we go from here? If you attack, we will fight. If you win, your win will be pyrrhic. Our former mother country and the world will defy you. I am fully aware that no other country, friendly or not, accepted your offers of kindness. We decline. I decline, John. Attack us, and Newland will share one similar trait with Imploria. We will both be islands."

John was furious. He had been rebuffed, insulted, and intellectually outmaneuvered. He said, "Thirty days, twenty-nine now, I will wait. I will not offend the ghost of Caesar."

Hernando replied, "My answer is no now, and it will be no then. Proceed accordingly, Sovereign."

John abruptly hung up the phone. He was determined to give Imploria the time his historic idols afforded their foes. The next day, John summoned Davis to his office and ordered him to contact Chilean authorities immediately. Davis began the process of obtaining Chilean permission to use their air space and waterways if hostilities were to ensue against Imploria. Chile granted this request for ships and airplanes, but the price was exorbitant. John agreed to their price without counter-offer. Newland had a modern but small navy and a small but potent air force. John asked Hinkins to prepare for an invasion and to be especially mindful that the vast majority of their forces were not members of the Sovereign Guard. The non-Sovereign Guard military was wary of Hinkins, so Hinkins ensured that non-guard generals were included in the plans. Hinkins also personally briefed his Sovereign Guard troops, who were eager to mobilize.

As the Sovereign of Newland prepared for action, his Implorian adversary began preparations as well. Hernando refused to be idle in light of Newland's threatened aggression.

Hernando reached out to Miruba for protection in addition to the United Nations for support. The United Nations passed a resolution with unanimous support, condemning any acts of aggression against Imploria. He was alone; the time was drawing near, and the pressure to decide on the path forward mounted with each passing day. As time progressed, more nations threatened sanctions against Newland. John was frustrated but still determined.

CHAPTER 25

The Angst Against Imploria

The twenty-ninth day after the offer arrived, neither party had changed its position. International pressure continued to mount against Newland in regard to its impending threat toward the fledgling island nation of Imploria. That morning, John arose and had coffee with Mary at their breakfast table. Mary was usually silent on matters of state but had proved to be a key ally in the discussions and actions involving the CBA. Unlike the CBA situation, John had not asked Mary for assistance with the Imploria decision. However, before he rose and left for the Sovereignty building, Mary inquired ever so softly, "John, how is the Imploria situation?"

John was pensive and restless in his response, "Not good. Hernando won't budge, and there's international pressure everywhere. All of Newland is watching and waiting. It's rough. I wish hostilities could be avoided."

Mary, thankful that John had finally communicated with her, said, "I understand."

He continued, "I've never liked war, or death, or all that. It's expensive. My plan was peaceful, fair, and made perfect sense. Hernando just would not accept it."

Mary thought briefly and spoke, "Call him. Sweeten the deal; ask if there is anything short of war he will agree to. Try riches, diplomacy, anything. I fear Miruba could engage if Newland attacks. John, that would be a disaster for our forces."

John knew Mary was correct. "My forces are in place and ready to move. I dread this. I will call him this morning. Mary, thank you." John took his final sip of coffee, kissed her, and began to depart.

She stopped him. "Dinner tonight?"

"No, not tonight unless we strike a deal. Thanks again."

He left for the Sovereignty Building with an entourage of ten Sovereign Guards and arrived ready to take action. Ironically, it was the first of the month—Carlene's meeting time. John rushed into his office, focused on the Imploria situation. Carlene had arrived early and was waiting for him. John looked up and saw his blissful brunette holding a mug of coffee for him. They hugged, and she sensed his tenseness.

"What, no kiss today, Sovereign?" She cooed at him.

John always relished an opportunity to kiss Carlene but was content with an awkward peck of a kiss on the cheek before he sat down.

Carlene asked, "Big day tomorrow, John?"

John glared at her, saying simply, "Yes."

Carlene leaned forward without pause or reserve and said, "Crush them, John. Make a statement. The world is watching, and now, you must act."

John was unmoved by her suggestion. He asked, "What about a final call, an outreach to Hernando?"

The bristling brunette stood and exclaimed, "Who is in control? This is an insult! The stage is set, John; the world will react to your actions."

"What about Newland's reputation internationally?" he exclaimed. "What about the Miruba? Will they attack us? Impose international sanctions? I can't even count on the Americans."

"The Americans," Carlene scoffed. "John, fear not, the Americans value money more than anything. We are Americans. Wake up. They won't lose profit or sleep over Imploria. Ignore their rhetoric. The massive American presence in Newland ensures they will do nothing."

John timidly responded, "Carlene, are you sure?"

Carlene affirmatively stated, "Yes, I'm positive. The Americans may moan, groan, and complain, but in the end, it's about dollars; it's always been about the dollars."

John pursued his uncertainty. "What about Miruba?"

With complete confidence, Carlene said, "Cut a deal. Imploria left them after giving them hell for years. Punish Imploria in a way that Miruba could not or would not do, and the mother country has a built-in excuse to appease its few remaining colonies."

After his discourse with Carlene, John finally felt emboldened in a way he had not experienced since the initial delivery of the letter to Hernando. Perhaps it was Carlene, or perhaps the emotional build-up of the thirty-day wait. Regardless, he was ready to take action. He thanked Carlene, they kissed, and she departed.

John summoned Hinkins to his office and ordered him to place a final call to Hernando. Hinkins's call reached Hernando's office, but Hernando refused to speak with him. Hinkins looked up at John for guidance.

John said, "Hang up. It's over. Well . . . I wish it were over, anyway."

Chapter 26

The Move Against Imploria

The sun rose over Imploria on a warm August morning. Daylight revealed three Newland destroyers off the coast of the island with several supporting naval craft. The skies above Imploria were dotted with aircraft: fighter jets, bombers, and navigation planes. Each aircraft was adorned with Newland's flag on their wings and tails. The airplanes flew back and forth over the relatively small area without using their munitions. It was an impressive show of force directed at Imploria, specifically Hernando. The destroyers aligned themselves parallel to the coast in the ready position. John was kept abreast of all formations by his efficient military commanders.

John was bold but still apprehensive about an all-out war. He continued to hope that Hernando would agree to his wishes. Rhetoric and debates had always been John's arsenal, but now, a conflict replete with casualties loomed over the Sovereign. John had remained awake many a night thinking about the potential loss of life due to his impending orders. Even in his domestic rule, John opted for exile or public humiliation over violence whenever possible. On occasion, his internal forces employed violence, but this was rare in Newland. In this view, John was a clear minority as his Sovereign Guard often pressed him to be more brutal in his orders when dealing with the occasional dissident or criminal.

Hinkins entered John's office, saying, "It's time, Sovereign."

John looked up at his most loyal servant. "Hinkins, you are loyal, obedient, and powerful. I know I can count on you to defend me, if necessary, to the death. What should I do?"

Hinkins, who had all of those qualities articulated by John, was also fierce and decisive. He advised his leader, "I think we should proceed, Sovereign. Immediately."

John, still unconvinced, continued, "Today, I am the aggressor. When I give the order, hundreds, perhaps more, will die. I have a deep problem with that."

Hinkins was surprised by his leader's hesitancy. John didn't say it, but he wished that in his hour of need, he had a scholar's advice, a thinker. Instead, he had a brutal but loyal thug bent on violence. John, resigned to his fate and the reality at hand, finally relented to his military muscleman. "Do it, Hinkins. Attack."

Hinkins, savoring the order, picked up the phone and gave the order to his military commander in Imploria. "Commence attack."

Hinkins looked at John, smiled wickedly, and said, "Done, sir. It is done." John slumped in his chair and looked sheepishly at his live-action screen, focusing on Imploria. Immediately, thunderous booms arose from his destroyers while Newland planes swarmed and dove toward Imploria's mainland. The devastation was thorough and swift. The response from Imploria's meager defensive force was minimal and ineffective.

Within an hour, the battle had completely and utterly devasted Imploria. Hernando had been in a bunker, relaying his primitive military orders without success. He emerged from his bunker to view the situation. The scenic island was ablaze, with massive piles of rubble adorning streets where century-old buildings once stood. Hernando wept uncontrollably.

Hernando's military, which a few years earlier had marched in the streets with him in valiant defiance of Miruba, was now in chaos and stood in sheer awe of the massive destruction to their homeland. Soldiers pleaded with Hernando to concede and surrender as the onslaught from the sea and air continued to rain down upon a seemingly defenseless Imploria. Hernando asked his top commander to assess the situation. The general said, "Mr. President, this is dire. Thousands are dead, and there are miles of complete ruin and continuing devastation."

Hernando inquired further, "General, if they continue to invade, can our troops repel them?"

"No, sir!" the general shrieked in panic. "The bombardments have devastated our ranks. We are beaten, sir."

Hernando understood. He gave another order. "General, get my phone."

The general said, "All communications are destroyed, sir. Worse, the hospitals were destroyed. Wounded and dead are piling up in the streets."

In frustration, Hernando screamed, "Get me a white T-shirt! Run it up the flagpole immediately. We must surrender."

The bombardment continued with unabated accuracy, each blast spewing rubble upon rubble. John, watching the carnage from his office on a widescreen, sat mortified and silent. He grew ill at the magnitude of the damage while Hinkins roared with enthusiasm as portions of Imploria fell into the sea under the relentless barrage. Suddenly, John eyed a white T-shirt flying in the wind on a flagpole atop Imploria's capital building.

John stood up. "Stop the attack! They are surrendering! See the white flag?"

Within seconds, the massive bombardment stopped. John ordered Hinkins, "Get me Hernando on the phone immediately."

Hinkins replied, "Sovereign, we will try. Communications are destroyed on the island. Our paratroopers have landed and are approaching their capital. Perhaps they can reach him."

As Newland troops rushed toward Imploria's capital, white flags flanked their pathways to the main square. Moments earlier, the Implorians were their foes, but now, the Newland military was on a mercy mission. The invaders saw rampant devastation, dead bodies, and body parts. Screaming and wounded Implorians were everywhere.

Hernando entered the main square to greet the invading Newland forces. "We surrender," he shouted. "Help us! Please, help my people."

A young officer reached Hernando first and spoke to the stricken leader. "We accept your surrender. Our Sovereign has ordered an immediate mercy mission."

Hernando, still in shock from the attack and the magnitude of the losses, could only repeat himself. "Help us, help us."

Miruba and the rest of the world did nothing except offer condemning language for the attack. Offers of aid were made from around the world to Imploria, but Hernando was personally devastated. The international community sat idly by while his nation was destroyed. John insisted on an immediate and thorough mercy mission for its newly conquered province. John insisted that all necessary resources be directed toward Imploria to aid the wounded and rebuild Newland's new territory—its new state.

John immediately flew to Imploria on his personal jet. Upon landing, he was sickened by the destruction he witnessed. Implorians wandered aimlessly among the ruins. Buildings had collapsed into dust, and the rubble and wreckage of ruined lives were scattered across the broken streets. Many Implorians stood and stared at the Newland invader as he rode in the backseat of a car through ravaged streets toward Imploria's Capitol Square. Upon arrival in the main square, he witnessed massive damage to every building. He exited his vehicle accompanied by his Sovereign Guards and reached his troops on the steps of the Capitol Building. They saluted their Sovereign. Newland's military had secured the entire island with only minimal assistance from Sovereign Guard troops.

The military commander saluted his Sovereign, and John inquired, "Where is Hernando?"

"Inside, sir," the commander said. John strode at a brisk pace into the building. He entered the main chancellery office and found a ruffled, shell-shocked Hernando motionless in his chair.

John barked at the beaten Hernando, "I tried to avoid all of this, you fool!"

Hernando remained silent.

John continued to rant, "Hernando, I demand you respond to me. This is not my fault. It's on you, damn you!"

Hernando looked up at his Newland conqueror and whimpered, "In three hours, you have destroyed centuries of work and killed thousands of people. I hope you are content. Imploria is now yours."

John tried to reason with the stricken leader. "I need you to rebuild Imploria with me. I tried this the easy way, and you refused. You own this, Hernando. I now demand you serve me and our people."

Hernando looked at John, bewildered by the lecture's insensitivity and timing. John remained oblivious to Hernando's personal devastation and bent on justifying himself for the losses. He continued, "We have unlimited wealth and resources. I will help you."

Hernando weakly responded, "What of the dead?"

"Bury them."

Hernando continued, "The tens of thousands of wounded?"

John replied, "We will treat them. As we speak, thousands of construction crews are in the air, on their way here to rebuild. Within twenty-four hours, we will begin reconstruction."

This did not console Hernando; he became silent anew.

John walked out of Hernando's office, found the young captain who had secured the square, and ordered him, "Fly our flag, Captain. Everywhere a white flag flies, fly the flag of Newland."

"Yes, Sovereign," the young officer said.

John drove away from the devastated Imploria, boarded his plane, and flew back to Newland. The press awaited him in droves, and the United Nations condemned him as international criticism poured in. John spoke with Davis, his Foreign Minister, and decided to attend a press conference. He was rattled, unsure, and internally upset with himself, and it showed. The Sovereign had his victory but could not revel in it.

The ornate and polished Sovereignty Building was a direct contrast to the Implorian Capitol Building, which he had just left in ruins. He approached the podium of the small and sparse briefing room seriously and subdued, speaking in an uncanny monotone that was alien to his demeanor.

"Today, we have a new state, Imploria, which has joined the nation of Newland. As of now, all Implorians enjoy the benefits of Newland citizenship. I sincerely hope the international community understands the significance of this merger and responds in a positive manner."

John nodded, thanked them, took no questions, and left the podium. He was done. The press was astounded by his brevity and reluctance to answer questions. They responded accordingly in their coverage. That evening, John received word from Imploria that Hernando had taken his own life. Imploria's liberator was dead, along with its short-lived independence. Upon receiving this news, John became violently ill.

CHAPTER 27

The Aftermath of Imploria

Over the next few weeks, casualty figures came in from the Imploria campaign. Twenty-five thousand dead, mostly civilians, and approximately fifty thousand wounded, also mostly civilians. Thousands on the island were still unaccounted for. On the Newland side, there were less than one hundred casualties. The margin of victory was overwhelming, and the recovery effort was in full swing.

Construction crews from Newland and beyond were hired to begin immediate and thorough reconstruction. John insisted on swift, efficient cleanup and rebuilding of the crushed nation. He knew the sooner the reconstruction was complete, the sooner the dire memories of the invasion and its horrific toll would fade. Retaliation fears were acutely on John's mind. He kept his military on full alert, especially in light of his fear of Imploria's former mother country. Nap Davis, the ever-clever and loyal Foreign Minister, began reaching out to the international community to attempt to initiate a healing process.

In the days following the conquest, John returned home sullen and withdrawn. He dined with Mary and their sons in noticeable silence. One evening, about three weeks after the surrender, Mary carefully inquired of John, "You've been quiet lately. Is it Imploria?"

John was surprised by her inquiry but still internally tortured by the loss of life and the aftermath of the campaign. He replied in an exhausted breath, "Yes, Mary. They never saw it coming."

Mary was surprised at her husband's naiveté but wanted to comfort him. She asked, "Is it getting any better?"

Her embattled spouse replied, "Yes, Mary, much better. We're rebuilding every day at a rapid pace, and so many of the wounded are healing and getting better." John caught himself in a moment of grieving enthusiasm. "But, Mary, the loss of life, what a horror, it was massive. I tried to avoid it, really, I did. I wanted to win, to show our strength, not this."

Mary was pleased that John was finally opening up and discussing his feelings. She prodded him, "Continue, please."

Ever reluctant to criticize John, Mary listened intently as he confessed his thoughts to her. Finally, John asked for her thoughts. "Mary, tell me what you think. I am tortured by all of this."

Mary smiled gently and spoke in a most soothing tone. "Well, that would take days. But, on Imploria, let's start there. John, that was a mistake; you know it, and I know it. We didn't need it."

John mildly protested, "But my offers to other countries . . . they were ignored. This should have been an easy yes for dozens of countries, and they just said no. Most of these nations are broke, corrupt, and backward. Newland is not. Their leaders came, showed respect and interest, and then said no. Sure, I forced it with Imploria, but they were better off as a colony than as a free state. Now, they are better off as a part of us."

Mary sighed. "Are they, John?"

John, more confident, professed his thoughts. "Of course they are. Colonization was beneficial for the colony and the colonized. The demise of colonization brought chaos, poverty, and a bastardized version of neocolonialism. Just new masters and worse effects."

Mary earnestly said, "Please explain. This is confusing."

John tried anew. "Well, take Imploria. For centuries, Miruba cared for it, protected it, and supported it. Then, one day, they were free, or so it seemed. They still needed Miruba for trade, currency, and protection. In reality, they were still a pawn."

Mary responded, "John, the people of Imploria were largely glad to be free. We crushed them. They may have been naive, John, but now, they are devastated."

John knew that Mary was not pleased with his victory in Imploria. He wanted to please her, so he asked, "What should I do?"

Mary was thankful for the earnest inquiry. She replied, "Be good to them. Feed them, nurture them, and help them regain some semblance of a people. This will ease their pain and yours."

John thought briefly and said, "I will. I promise. I've already started, but I will continue. The aid will be massive."

John, relieved, finally had his first full night of sleep in over forty-five days. Mary, though still disappointed, was content. She knew John would meet with his Cabinet the next day to discuss the future of Newland's new state. This would be, of course, after his monthly scheduled meeting with Carlene.

Chapter 28

The Afterglow of Imploria

John arose and arrived at his office early the next day. He was no longer as morose as he had been but was not gleeful either. Carlene arrived at nine, bold and beautiful. They met alone, and she greeted him as a conquering hero.

"John, great job!" she exclaimed. He paused as she hugged him. "You crushed them! Hernando—that fraud—and his band of peasant freedom fighters."

John listened to the only person who had given him any acclaim for the Imploria campaign. Carlene treated the entire ordeal as if it were a trivial sporting match. She flippantly inquired, "What's for breakfast? I'm starved."

John was surprised by her cavalier approach to this event but answered her request, "Eggs, toast, and hollandaise for you, my dear, your favorite."

Carlene replied, "Let's eat," and teased her host with feigned sincerity, "So, whom do we conquer next?"

John was aghast but refused to show it. She laughed aloud and chided him further, "Okay, no more lands for now. I'll settle for a new hotel on Imploria. The Sovereign is fine, but a change in venue would be nice."

Newland was in full swing in its sixth year, and Carlene had been a regular for quite some time. John adored her company and doted on her in a manner observed by many but never commented on. John thought her request for a hotel in a land that was still reeling from devastation was a lark, but she was serious. She put down her coffee and spoke. "Name it after me, John—the Hotel Carlene. I don't want excuses; a simple yes will suffice. Think of it: the Hotel Carlene on Newland's new province of Imploria."

John, distraught but determined to please Carlene, said, "What an interesting idea. I'll look into it at once."

Indifferent to John's internal turmoil, Carlene finished her breakfast, kissed him goodbye, and departed.

At ten o'clock, John held his first Cabinet meeting since the Imploria campaign. The Ministers convened without much fanfare. John opened the meeting with an invitation for questions. Jones, the ever-eager and successful Minister of Commerce, inquired, "Sovereign, have you seen the numbers on the economic progress in Imploria?"

"Not yet, Jones," John said. "Update me."

Jones stood and elaborated, "Sovereign, we have invested millions of dollars in the month since acquiring our new state. Construction is booming, with buildings, streets, coastline revitalization, and a new hospital. Of course, this investment will ultimately be profitable, but it will take some time."

John stood and spoke, "Good work, Jones. I knew I could count on you. Imploria must have the same grandeur as Newland proper. It is ours now. What about a new hotel?"

Jones, a bit startled by this inquiry, said, "Fortunately, the Imploria Hotel was not harmed during the campaign. It was on a part of the island that was largely left intact."

"I see." John immediately changed his line of questioning to the next important topic on his mind. "Jones, have any of the sanctions affected us?"

Jones answered, "Minimally at best, Sovereign, other countries have filled the gaps. We are fine. With the Newland renaissance in Imploria, trade will actually increase, sir." He cleared his throat and then continued, "The Americans, sir, may take a while to respond fully, but once they get over their feigned attempt at outrage over Imploria, they will be fine. Their state department is already reaching out to Davis to push their world benevolence rhetoric. In the end, it's always dollars over dogma, greed over grievance, and opportunity over outrage."

"I hope so!" John exclaimed. "I want our American brethren back in the fold."

Burnakov, the Russian, could not resist the moment. "Sovereign, have they ever been in the fold?" he inquired.

John was silent and merely leered at his czarist minister. All others remained silent. John felt a burning desire to address the American position. "Jones, you are a Canadian, Burnakov, a Russian. I, like some others in the room, am American." The ministers all looked up at their Sovereign. He continued, "You've got to be inherently American to understand this, but America's worldview is sincere. I know this; I felt this. At one time, I legislated this. When all else fails in the pursuit of human goodness, it's always the Americans who revive and honor what's best about mankind. It's hard to explain and even harder to quantify, but it is eternal. America is the bastion of freedom and human dignity."

The Cabinet grew silent and motionless. They had heard their Sovereign profess many doctrines or causes in speeches, lectures, and actions, but they had never experienced their absolute ruler's wrath in favor of his former country. If only for a second, the Sovereign's heart bled red, white, and blue in a land of seemingly only black and white.

John realized his lapse into American patriotism left his Cabinet at a loss for words, so he pivoted quickly by complimenting Jones and his minions. "Anyhow, my friends, good work in Imploria and beyond."

The Cabinet felt a sense of instant relief as John diffused his rhetoric. The meeting proceeded and then concluded without further incident.

As the ministers departed, John asked Jones and Sands, the Tourism Minister, to stay behind. "Gentlemen," he said, "Great meeting and great work."

They were relieved.

John added, "I think we need a new hotel in the heart of New Imploria."

Both Jones and Sands readily agreed. Sands said, "I gave you the Sovereign and La Verdad. Sovereign, what shall I build for you now?"

John looked at his Commerce and Tourism Ministers and replied, "Call it 'The Carlene,' and build it in twelve months."

Sands responded with a smile, "Sovereign, I will build it in eight."

John nodded with pleasure, and the ministers departed. John sat alone in his office. He sighed and closed his eyes, attempting to rest after the awkward Cabinet session. The next day, the Americans unilaterally released all sanctions against Newland. John thought deeply about this action and wondered to himself whether Jones and Burnakov were correct. He knew he should have been thrilled about the lifting of sanctions in light of Newland's most recent actions. However, a perverse sadness came upon him as he assessed his conscience. The Sovereign finally ordered his Minister of Information to issue a press release praising the lifting of sanctions and accentuating the swift and massive rebuilding efforts in Imploria. All was back to normal in Newland, or so it seemed.

CHAPTER 29

Newland Throws a Seven

The seven-year anniversary of Newland was less than a month away. Huge celebrations were planned all over the country. The international sting of the Imploria campaign had somewhat faded, and, in fact, John stressed the need for the island state of Newland to participate fully in the festivities. Schools, sports facilities, and even hospitals were all poised to enjoy the pomp and circumstance of Newland.

Imploria had been totally rebuilt at an enormous cost to Newland. Al profited, as usual, as did Carlene, but on a balance sheet, Newland's losses were staggering. John was determined to restore Imploria as best he could, regardless of cost. This was a mission driven by tremendous internal guilt, even though it was marketed as a great investment in Newland's future.

The Carlene, though smaller than the Sovereign Hotel, was equally as elegant and cost twice as much to construct as the La Verdad. It was open for business and was as popular as its sister hotels in Newland proper. A special anniversary party was set at the hotel with foreign dignitaries and affluent guests. Despite the ebb and flow of Newland's status in the eyes of the international community, foreign dignitaries accepted Newland's invitation to celebrate.

John summoned his Cabinet, ever loyal and optimistic, and ordered them to prepare an additional five-year plan for Newland. Some of the ministers were privately surprised, as the country was still exceeding expectations in all sectors. The economy was strong and growing, and crime was virtually non-existent. Even the weather had cooperated, with ideal conditions for Newland's agricultural industry. Imploria's governor, who was personally appointed by John, was a vocal supporter of Newland and an ardent advocate for Newland proper. John was surprised but pleased that there was no active resistance toward Newland in Imploria. Newland's surveillance of its new state confirmed the quietude of the great state of Imploria.

The festivities leading up to the country's anniversary were in full swing, and the mood in Newland was positive and extremely patriotic. Nationalism was rampant in Newland, as it was entwined with the Ideal State's nature. One evening, about a week before the actual anniversary, Al arrived late at the Sovereignty Building. He often arrived unannounced but was always welcomed. John was meticulously drafting his five-year plan with his ministers in tow. He was confident again and exceedingly pleased as the data from every sector of society was consistently improving. Growth and success seemed unrestrained. John hoped to continue with his framework for continued prosperity.

Al approached John in his office. The Sovereign was accompanied by massive, black-clad Sovereign Guards, who appeared as mighty pillars of loyalty to their leader. Al greeted them all and, in a rare display of formality, addressed John by his title. "Sovereign, may we have a minute to chat privately?"

The guards and ministers raised their heads at this request, but John diffused the moment with his reply, "Sure, Al, glad to chat with you. Let's walk and talk."

As the two men walked alone in the palatial Sovereignty Building, Al said in a serious and sullen tone, "It's about CBA."

John grew still and ceased walking. He looked directly at Al and lamented, "Not them again."

Al tried to console the man who had made him billions. "Yes, it's them, and they want another meeting—soon."

John, aching with frustration over the situation, exclaimed, "Tell the three wise men I'll meet. Let's get it over with as soon as possible. I want nothing to ruin our seventh anniversary."

Al paused and responded quietly, "Well, John, I wish it were that simple. It's not just Combs, Burns, and Amos."

Puzzled, John grimaced. "Who else?"

Al did not hesitate, "All of them, John. Apparently, all of CBA's investors want to meet with you."

John stood still, remaining silent as an eerie sense of wariness gripped him. He finally asked, "Al, who are they?"

Shaking his head, Al could only respond, "Maybe we will finally find out."

John pointed his finger at Al and demanded again, "Set the meeting as soon as possible. No more fear. Just you, me, and them. It's time to confront whoever or whatever they are."

Al just nodded his assent and walked off. John stood alone amidst the grandeur of his Sovereignty Building. The meeting he had long dreaded was going to convene, and his overwhelming emotion was loneliness. He decided to go home to Mary and his children.

Later, Al informed John that the CBA had agreed to a meeting in Newland on the day before the seventh anniversary. That night, as he had done for countless nights in his role as Sovereign, John lay awake, pondering his fate and that of his beloved Newland. The CBA had always been a mystery—nebulous people, unstated goals, intermittent involvement. John had thought and thought, over and over, the same quandary. *Who are they?* He blamed himself for not demanding more information about them in their original negotiations, but for now, that point was moot. In John's view, he had conquered the challenges of forming and running the ideal state and bringing Newland the international acclaim it deserved. Now, once again, he had to answer for his actions to the CBA. John decided to determine, once and for all, whether the CBA was a friend or foe, a partner or a pariah.

The Sovereign still battled his omnipresent loneliness. He finally resolved that a ruler of any nation would ultimately have to face the difficult decisions of governing alone. Caesars had done it, emperors, kings, even prime ministers and presidents. He decided that his moment of decision had arrived, and he, too, would rise to the occasion.

Despite the onset of his self-pity, John prayed every day. He was still a committed Christian. His view of Christianity entailed Roman Catholicism sprinkled with strains of protestant evangelical fervor. It brought John a sense of contentment in light of his place in the Earthly realm. John knew he was not free from sin but balanced his sins with his self-perceived attributes and committed himself to the conclusion that he, like Newland, was far ahead in the saint versus sinner equation. He devoted himself daily to prayer for forgiveness as he was reluctant to discuss any of his perceived frailties with others.

John knew his predicament with the CBA could potentially be problematic. But, in his view, he was just, humble, and enlightened. John was ready to play the role of the Sovereign in front of a much different audience. Finally, he decided to seek outside counsel to ease his woes.

As John considered his list of possible advisors, he immediately ruled out Al Grudger. Seven years had shown Al to be one-sided—his side. His greed and self-interest almost made his D.C.-based father seem altruistic. Al was present but untouchable. The thought of Carlene entered his mind for this task, but John concluded that her brutal and uncaring approach to the Imploria campaign had harmed him in far too many ways. He made his final decision: he would speak to three people—his priest, Father Managgio, Hinkins, head of his Sovereign Guard, and Mary.

Mary, as his wife, was first. They convened over a cup of coffee in the kitchen. He asked, "Mary, do you remember the CBA?"

Mary responded in a surprised tone, "Yes, they're your financiers, right?"

John replied, "Yes, of sorts."

Mary clarified, "They gave you the money to start Newland."

"That's right, and, well, they're back."

Mary was not only bright and intuitive; she had an excellent memory for details. She had sensed John's tenseness of late and found it odd in light of the upcoming anniversary. She pressed him, "It was Combs, Burns, and Amos, right? Left us alone for a while, returned, disappeared again, and now they have reemerged?"

"Yes, but it's worse. It's not just Combs, Burns, and Amos. It's all of them."

Mary inquired further, "All of whom?"

"That's just it—I don't know. That's my dilemma. Al says—"

She interrupted him, "Oh no, not Al."

"Mary, he's just the messenger, just their conduit. He says the entire group of investors wants to meet. I agreed. I have to."

Mary sat at the kitchen table and considered what he'd said. She remained silent for several minutes before speaking. John listened intently. "Don't trust Al. He will be more than a messenger in this meeting. If he perceives loss or gain, he will react accordingly and leave you hanging. His loyalty is to himself. Watch him." John remained silent, waiting for her next dose of advice. She obliged. "As for the group, listen very carefully, observe them, then think before you speak. You are the Sovereign of a nation. You chose to accept a deal from people you did not know and probably acted too hastily. Now, you must react, but only after you gain more facts."

John felt obliged to speak. "I never get all the facts from them, sometimes no information at all. I get vague questions and vague answers. It's unreal. They remind me of the Greek Gods of myth—intrusive, temperamental, and seemingly all-powerful but unclear. I am so concerned."

Mary insisted, "Trust your instincts. After you hear them out, flush them out."

John hugged her tightly and thanked her. He was not only sincere but genuinely thankful for her. As he began to depart, Mary whispered, "Please, John, don't listen to her."

The sheepish Sovereign replied, "Who?"

Mary chided him for the first time. "You know who, John—Carlene."

He blushed a red tone so deep that it was apparent to both of them he was bathing in embarrassment. She refused to back off this topic. "I know you meet with her. She's dangerous, very dangerous. I've never understood the hold she has on you, but it's there."

John, turning redder as the conversation progressed, said, "Mary, I love you, always have, always will. You are my wife, the First Lady of Newland. You are it."

Mary was not yet content to rest as years of pent-up frustration with John finally erupted. John had dreaded the conversation with the CBA, but at least he had the chance to prepare. He did not anticipate this line of discourse with Mary and had tried desperately to avoid it.

But much to his dismay, Mary continued, "Perhaps, John, but whenever you speak with her, something happens. Beware: from the Caesars to Napoleon to you, and even the quiet, unassuming men of the world who live, work, and die without a whimper, there is always one—one woman who, for whatever reason, grasps their essence, affects their being, and enslaves their very souls. I fear Carlene is that to you and, therefore, is my nemesis, too."

John, still aghast but too contrite to be angered by his wife's accusations, sat silent. Mary looked at him in a rare but aggressive way, hoping to elicit a response. When one was not forthcoming, she resumed, "I will help you always. My only ask for now is that you deny her in your hour of need. She is poison, pure poison."

John looked at his wife, though filled with an ocean of guilt in his soul, and merely replied, "I'll be careful."

Mary nodded and left John at the kitchen table to reflect on her words. John knew Mary was correct in every criticism she had of him and his obsession with Carlene. His guilt was memorialized in the Implorian hotel, The Carlene, named after her for the entire world to see. It seemed that Imploria was the site of more than one pyrrhic victory for John.

Fewer than ten minutes had passed since John's conversation with Mary when Father Managgio, his priest, arrived. Managgio was strong, Italian, and devoutly spiritual. He was John's personal priest and, from the beginning, had not been judgmental toward the Sovereign or Newland. Managgio was not only a priest to John but was also his friend. However, he had never been his mentor or adviser on issues of State. Matters of faith had been his venue, and John had been comfortable with that relationship.

John greeted Managgio, kissed his ring, and, in a sincere sign of respect, hugged the elder Monsignor. Managgio, at least twenty years John's senior, sensed the Sovereign's dower mood. "What ails you, my son?" he inquired.

"So much, Father, so much."

Managgio spoke with authority and confidence to a man whose own words were typically associated with those qualities. "God can handle everything, heal everything."

John, unaffected by his priest's words, launched into his woes. "There's a group coming to see me, Father. They gave me the money and resources necessary to found Newland. Now, they are coming."

Managgio asked, "Coming for what, my son?"

John leaned forward and said, "I don't know, Father. That's what ails me. They show up from time to time, more bothersome than not, and never specific."

"Continue, my son," Managgio pressed.

"Three of them, three very odd men. Now, they all want to meet with me. I agreed, Father, but I'm ill-prepared."

The aged abbot thought deeply, then spoke to his parishioner, "So, as I understand it, you took money from a group of people you never knew and still don't. You must meet with them—press them for details, their roots, their purposes. If they are just, they will answer and work with you. If they are not, oh, John, I fear for you."

John was concerned, more concerned than ever. He inquired, "What do you mean, Father?"

Managgio tried, "Evil, my son, is always evil. It may mask itself, morph itself, or even attempt to recreate itself. John, if this is evil, you must fight it."

John kneeled before Managgio and pleaded with him, "Father, how will I know if they are evil? Am I just? Am I good?"

Managgio responded, "John, I believe you are just and good, but history may not view you in that regard."

John exclaimed, "Father, you are as illusive in your judgment as the CBA is in their motives!"

"I'll leave the final judgment to God, my son. For now, you will have to concede to the historians."

John leered at Managgio and grew bolder, "Father, sometimes the world needs a historical son of a bitch to set it straight! I might be just that. Father, please, pray for me."

The wise priest had served his purpose. As he got up to leave, in a parting word, he cautioned the unsteady leader. "Heaven and Hell are full of historical sons of bitches. Where they land is up to them. Follow a good heart, a good soul, and pray. If you fail, son, a new level of Hell may await you."

John, angling for a position of hope, asked, "And if I succeed?"

The priest smiled, "Perhaps a corner office in heaven occupied by a handful of world leaders."

"Thank you, Father," John said. "God bless you."

John was exhausted physically and emotionally. His wife and priest had both weighed in on his impending meeting, and the strain was weighing heavily upon him. Finally, Hinkins arrived. "Sovereign, I am here to serve you," he said.

Hinkins stood at attention. He could be harsh but also thoughtful and had always been among John's most ardent, loyal followers. John asked Hinkins to be at ease and sit; the rigid general complied but would have been more comfortable standing. Hinkins asked, "How may I serve my Sovereign?"

"It's the CBA again."

Hinkins responded, "I offered to slay those three leeches years ago. You stopped me, Sovereign."

John nodded his head and said, "Yes, you did, and I did stop you, but there are more of them. Several more are coming to Newland to meet with me."

Hinkins, assuming his role as the Sovereign's gladiator, did not hesitate to aid him. He blurted out, "Shall I kill them all, sir?"

Perplexed, John responded, "I wish it were that easy. I don't know who they are, who they represent, what they want, or why. It's a plague, an amorphous attack. What should I do?"

Hinkins was decisive. He said, "Sovereign, may I stand?"

John nodded in the affirmative.

"Thank you, Sovereign. You must realize every one of them is your foe. Trust nothing. Be alert. Then, convene with your most able and loyal followers and defeat them."

John, though listening intently, was unconvinced. "Hinkins," he said, "I wish it were that easy. These are powerful, wealthy people who hide the truth from me and Newland."

Hinkins, in an almost admonishing tone, advised his leader, "Sovereign, lie to them. Deceive them. Use whatever means you deem necessary to defeat them."

John stood and looked directly at his most loyal military commander. "I built this nation, Newland, on truth, honesty, and all that is inherently good in humankind. How can I deviate from this formula now?"

Hinkins disagreed with his Sovereign. "No, Sovereign, you built Newland on strength, power, money, and people. Sir, if you will permit me, you have built it on a lie."

John was stunned to hear such a candid but different assessment of the foundations of his ideal state. He inquired further, "Hinkins, please explain."

Hinkins gladly obliged. "These CBA people allowed you, no, encouraged you to construct a country. They held something back. I don't know what, but they have hidden something critical, something crucial to you and Newland. Dishonest as they may have been, you accepted their premises and their lack of conditions. Sir, you assumed sincerity and truth and have erred in this assumption. Now, our nation's fate and yours, sir, rests in their hands."

John looked down and, in a desperate inquiry, asked, "Any chance they are honest?"

"No, sir," he replied.

John continued, "Maybe they will reason with us."

"Not likely, sir," Hinkins replied. "Sovereign, you cherish the truth. You live that way and rule that way. You expect that of others. I admire that, but, sir, it's a fallacy. Newland is pure, wholesome, and honest like it's Sovereign. These CBA people are not. I, too, fear them."

John stood silent for a few minutes and then thanked Hinkins, shook his hand, and dismissed him. John then sat at his desk pondering his next move when a letter arrived for him. The CBA would bring thirty people to the meeting. *Thirty to one*, he thought. He was filled with a sense of arcane heroism as he envisioned the meeting. He alone would bear the responsibility to face the foggiest of foes. The Sovereign was alone to chart the course of Newland's fate.

Chapter 30

The Meeting of the Mines

In the days surrounding Newland's seventh anniversary, John experienced an emotional rollercoaster. On the upside, the celebrations continued in honor of Newland's seventh anniversary. On the downside, the impending meeting with the CBA was fast approaching. As part of the festivities, John flew to Imploria for a celebration at The Carlene. John felt a sense of obligation to be there in light of Newland's history with Imploria. He wanted a huge party.

John arrived in Imploria at noon and greeted its new governor, Ibarra. Throngs of well-wishers lined the streets of Newland's only state, waving flags, singing songs, and praising their Sovereign and nation. Where shell-shattered landmarks and wounded Implorians had lined the streets just a few years earlier, modern highways and beauty now abounded.

The leaders met at The Carlene, which was ever so elegant, bold, and immaculate, like its namesake. After greeting Ibarra, John greeted Carlene, who was at her hotel to preside over the festivities. She was in full pomp, accepting the accolades of the visiting guests and patriots. Many attendees wondered why their Sovereign had named the impressive haven after her, but no one questioned the choice publicly. Noon arrived, and John was still conflicted despite the festivities surrounding him. The overflowing gala at The Carlene filled him with pride and joy, yet the upcoming meeting with the CBA gnawed at him, causing inescapable dread.

Interrupting his thoughts, Carlene chose that moment to walk over to John and honor herself amid the nation's nationalistic fervor. She quipped, "Did you bring me a gift, Sovereign?"

John gestured around at the lavish structure they were in and replied, "Thought I did," as the glittering "The Carlene" sign beamed across the ballroom.

Surprised at his witty retort, Carlene was not to be outquipped. "Oh, well, rain checks and rulers—the story of my life," she laughed. Sensing he was more pensive than usual, Carlene pressed him, as was her habit. "John, let's have fun and enjoy this moment. You can conquer the world tomorrow and make a train run on time next week. For now, relax and savor your empire."

John, who normally acquiesced to her whims, grew silent. Carlene was irked. "Okay, I'll let you win this time, but just this once. You have five minutes to tell me what's bothering you. Then, this is my day, my moment, my hotel, and my celebration with my Sovereign."

Forgoing Mary's advice, John confided his woes to Carlene. "Remember the CBA?" he inquired. He proceeded to bring her current on their actions and his predicament. She listened inattentively as she'd never appraised the CBA threat at the same level John and his minions had. Her minimal allotment of time devoted to him in his time of need was consistent with the minimal amount of affinity shown to him throughout their relationship. In a rare move, he reminded her of her scoffing at his opportunity to build Newland at its inception years earlier.

Carlene was surprised at John's discourse but wanted to move beyond his maudlin situation. She said, "John, enough of that. Let me make this easy for you. Meet with them, listen to them, and then dictate the terms of any agreement. What can they do? Nothing. You are Sovereign, Newland is booming, and you are all-powerful. They must be jealous. Who cares? You are in control."

John replied, "That is too simplistic."

Carlene brushed back her hair and spoke again, "I disagree. Tell them you are John Kinley, you alone are Sovereign over Newland, and neither you nor Newland will beckon to anyone. Now, I'm done. Honor me at my party."

Carlene walked away along a brilliant red carpet with a golden *C* crest on it that ran across the center of the hotel's ballroom. She was content. John, however, was not. Newland had rolled into the completion of its seventh year. John partook in the festivities, more as a spectator than as a Sovereign. The gala was tremendous. Newland was, for the moment, still the Ideal State.

At the night's conclusion, John kissed Carlene. Guiltily, he thought briefly of Mary and her admonitions. However, he knew that there was something about Carlene that affected him differently than any other person. Rather than fight it, he resigned himself to his frailty and headed home to Newland.

In no time, the day of the CBA meeting arrived. John wore his favorite navy suit and a new solid blue tie—a gift from Mary. Upon his arrival at the Sovereignty Building, Hinkins and two Sovereign Guards escorted him to their meeting venue, a sparse chamber officially called the Rubicon Room. They offered to remain with their leader, but John insisted they go. He ordered them to show the CBA guests in upon arrival and then to depart but remain close.

At nine o'clock sharp, thirty CBA members entered the meeting chamber. The Rubicon Room was filled with desks and chairs for the visitors. John stood at the front podium as twenty-five men and five women filed into the room. Combs, Burns, and Amos led the delegation. All thirty donned the same grey attire, proper and firm in appearance. John watched this show of unnerving uniformity and decided to leave his podium and shake every visitor's hand. As the Sovereign approached and greeted his ominous guests, they glared at him. John smiled with his usual charismatic charm, which fell flat upon the sterile leers of his onlookers. They were abrupt but polite, as even the original trio of Combs, Burns, and Amos acquiesced in the mutual show of introductions.

John, feeling an acute sense of loneliness, returned to the podium bent on addressing the CBA team. His strategy was to be proactive in a room where he felt defenseless. The room grew silent, and he addressed his guests.

"Welcome to Newland," he said with a trepidation everyone could sense. "As most of you know, I am John Kinley, Sovereign of Newland."

As he spoke, John carefully looked across the room, searching for a collective mood or demeanor. There was only silence and glares. He could not ascertain any emotions. He decided to feign self-confidence with a smile and rhetoric, which had moved millions to loyalty. As his speech continued to fall upon seemingly deaf ears and emotionless eyes, he changed course abruptly in an attempt to evoke some kind of a response. He spoke without smiling, reverting to his basic instincts clothed in honesty. "Please, ask me anything you wish. I'll tell you the truth, always the truth. Surely, you must have some questions. I would be more than happy to oblige."

Combs stood up as all eyes, including John's, pivoted to the CBA spokesman. "John, we are not pleased," he stated harshly.

John inquired, "About what, sir? What is displeasing to you?"

Combs continued, "I'm talking about the entire venture—you have failed, failed miserably."

The other twenty-nine attendees nodded in perfect unison. They were united in their message of disapproval.

Perplexed, John responded, "Surely, you kind people jest. Newland has accomplished in seven years what emperors have never attained. We lead the world in growth, have eliminated most of the blemishes of human frailty from the body politic, and still progress daily."

Combs abruptly interrupted John, rejecting the leader's attempt to curry favor with his gathering. He chided John anew, "As I said, you have been an abysmal failure, and we are not pleased. Save your remedial rhetoric for your mindless masses. We are totally displeased with our experiment."

John, ever the optimist, sensed his positive attitude waning in light of the verbal attack from Combs. He tried again. "Please, anyone in this room, ask me questions about anything that displeases you. I will answer."

Despite his pleas, Combs continued his relentless barrage on the befuddled Sovereign. "If we had questions, we would have asked. You must go. If you insist on a question, here it is: *when will you go?*"

The eyes of the CBA members locked onto the stunned ruler of Newland. John was shocked by this demand. He immediately pushed back. Raising his voice for the first time in adamant defiance, he exclaimed, "Mr. Combs, let me be clear: I did not anticipate a warm and friendly meeting with your group. However, I'd hoped it might be pleasant, but I was wrong. I accommodated you to be polite and fair, but your demands are ridiculous and border on the outrageous."

Combs stoically interrupted him, "Point of order, John. You don't accommodate us; we accommodate and control you." He lashed out further with a sinister but controlled grin. "You, sir, are fortunate that we afforded you the privilege of a meeting. My group can attest that we have been far less accommodating to others in many of our other ventures. Consider yourself fortunate—lucky, if you will. Choose a date and depart. That is all."

More defiant than ever, John refused to buckle under the CBA's pressure. He shouted at them, pounding on the podium, "Just who do you think you are? I have no idea who you are, what you are, or why you have come here! How dare you come into my country and demand I leave? To date, I have been polite, candid, and always available. Today, your group has presented hostilities to Newland and me. I will react accordingly."

Combs replied in his distinct monotone, "You and your Romans love a thirty days' notice, so how about that? After thirty days, we, too, will react accordingly. Remember, John, we tried to warn you."

John rebuked them again, "Tried? Really? Tried what? To show up and oust me? Let everyone in this room be on notice. This place, Newland, is a paradise—politically and in every other way."

Combs shook his head and addressed the ranting ruler of Newland, "Kinley, you don't understand. You are finished, done. The experiment is over."

"What is this? A shakedown? Is that it? If it's money you want, we can negotiate."

Combs stood silent; he did not respond.

John offered again, "If it's money you want, we can arrange a payment plan—your investment plus interest. I will not allow you or anyone to come to my country, my land, and take away the resources we possess. Your one trillion investment has returned trillions. You know it, I know it, and the world knows it."

Combs replied, "No, John, it's over."

John grew bolder as his arguments proved fruitless. He roared, "I made this place! I'll defend this place! My people will stand with me and defend it!"

Combs sat down, showing not only displeasure with John but the discussion. He spoke one final time, "John, go now or feel our wrath. Leave now, or your people will decry the day they chose Newland. You have thirty days."

John continued to try to engage them as the CBA ensemble stood up and began to walk out of the room. He shouted, "I banish you, you bastards! I banish you from Newland, from Imploria, and I owe you nothing! I offer you nothing! Be gone from our midst forever! You are a scourge, a plague. I strike you from the annuls of Newland history! You are gone, a nullity."

As Combs departed the room with Burns and Amos in tow, he looked back at John, adorning an evil grin. "At least you are entertaining."

John watched them depart, and he sank into a nearby chair, ill with fear. The meeting he had dreaded went far worse than he had imagined. His honesty and temper resulted in an all-out confrontation. If loneliness were a virtue, John was blessed in a bath of isolation, drenching his existence. If confusion were a sin, John had been damned to face an amorphous foe. After hours of self-consolation and thought, he arose from his chair and decided to enjoy the next day, Newland's seventh birthday. He wondered if it would be Newland's last.

CHAPTER 31

The Birthday Bashed

The next day, Newland's anniversary day, was bright and beautiful. A cool but refreshing wind swept across Capital City for the final day of a month-long celebration. Newlanders were enjoying the festivities, unaware of the looming threat posed by the CBA. John had not slept, lying awake with worry and fear in light of his disastrous meeting with the CBA. In fact, his plight was so bad that he could not even speak with Mary. He lay awake but silent all night, unable to communicate. He decided to allow Newland to celebrate the day but to inform the nation of its potentially impending doom later in the evening. In the morning, he gulped down his coffee with Mary, kissed her, and departed for his office without saying a word.

Newland's ministers were at the Sovereignty Building when John arrived; they were giddy with excitement. In their view, Newland had flourished for seven years, had an ambitious five-year plan, and all indicators were rosy with optimistic fervor. John allowed the celebration to continue throughout the day. He wanted his nation and his people to savor their past, as he was about to share news with them that would jeopardize their future.

With a heavy heart, John asked his Cabinet to be present for his five o'clock address to the nation. With everyone assembled in the People's Chamber that evening, the Sovereign solemnly approached the podium. The crowd was jubilant, applauding wildly as their leader began his remarks.

John began his speech, this time without notes or outlines; his only framework was survival. "Seven years ago today, we launched an endeavor together, a masterpiece of mankind, a nation unlike any other nation."

The crowd roared with approval but quickly noticed that their Sovereign was sullen and serious. "Please, do not applaud or celebrate further," he exclaimed, "for I have some disturbing news."

The crowds grew silent. John continued, "My loyal friends and ministers, you have been an inspiration to me and our countrymen. I have always been honest with you and with Newland. Now, I must share some difficult news with you. A group of people has threatened Newland. They met with me yesterday, thirty of them, and threatened to do us harm."

There were gasps and awe-struck gazes from the crowd as John enlightened them. The Cabinet drew close together with Hinkins up front.

John explained, "I know not their motives or desires. They call themselves the CBA. The only thing I know is that they have threatened our nation with unspecified drastic harm. I felt compelled to share this with you and to ask for your unified assistance against this peril."

Glitz, the Minister of Information, stepped forward from his seat in the front row and spoke aloud, "I speak for all here, my Sovereign, when I say we will do anything for you and Newland."

Thunderous applause arose from the crowds of onlookers who were still stunned by this revelation.

John humbly nodded his thanks and continued, "I shall order every department, every ministry, including our defense forces, to be on full alert at once."

John further informed the crowd that he and his ministers would begin meeting immediately. He thanked them and returned to his office in the Sovereignty Building. Newland was on notice; the Ideal State was under siege, as was its sovereign leader.

The mood inside the Sovereignty Building was serious but committed. Every minister was present and ready to assist their Sovereign and their beloved Newland, including two new members whose Cabinet posts were added with the addition of Imploria. John insisted that the people be kept abreast of the situation. Even in despair, the truth was paramount to him.

Jones, the Minister of Commerce, voiced his immediate concerns that the Newland financial markets, which were among the strongest and most stable in the world, would see devastation at this news. Jones told his Sovereign warily, "Sir, this is going to hurt us badly."

John instructed Jones to use Newland's abundant reserves to bolster its markets if necessary. Jones, though surprised, agreed to comply with his Sovereign's orders.

John sensed impending despair arising amongst his Cabinet members. "You fifteen are my most loyal public servants," John encouraged them. "The fate of Newland rests in your able hands, hearts, and minds."

Glitz, the Minister of Information, said, "As I said earlier, we are all with you, but Jones is correct, sir. If we divulge everything to the public, there will be panic, fleeing, and chaos. I implore you to use discretion in the dissemination of information. Sovereign, we are at war with an elusive enemy."

John was resolute in his position, "My friends, I am Sovereign. I have the obligation to rule as I see fit, and I shall. We must keep our legislators and citizens updated and aware of our plight, whether it improves or not. Let us resolve to inform, prepare, fight, and win."

There was silence at the Sovereign's dictate; obedience, but silence. John instructed Glitz to arrange an immediate national address on the radio. Glitz informed him of this peril, as news would spread through the international community. Friends and foes would know of Newland's woes.

John was undeterred. With his Cabinet by his side, he walked to the Sovereignty Building radio studio immediately. Over the radio, he told his citizens, "Today, my fellow citizens, I informed several of our countrymen of a threat to our nation, our people, and our way of life. I want each and every citizen of Newland to know that your public servants and I are on full alert and will combat the enemy known only as 'the CBA.' I ask for your assistance as we wage an all-out war against these nebulous but foreign invaders. I know not how the CBA plans to attack us, fight us, or oppose us. I assure you that we are resolved to achieve total victory against this foe, and we will return to our proud and prosperous way of life in Newland. I ask you to return to your homes, pray harder, dream bigger, and above all, remain united."

Glitz never left John's side. After his address, John was direct with his propaganda chief, "Get information flowing to the people. Instill insight and patriotism, not panic."

John knew that Glitz would be critical in the battle against the CBA. Holding the loyalty and hopes of the people together as the fight ensued would be essential. Nap Davis, the Foreign Minister, was directed to contact Newland's best allies first and reach out for international assistance. Davis agreed and began his outreach immediately.

Hinkins, head of the Sovereign Guard, and Jacobs, the Defense Minister, sat with John to plan for potential military action. Both men had proven their loyalty to John and Newland prior to this time, but this new challenge would test their relationships. Jacobs sat facing John and Hinkins with a stern expression. He practiced awkward politeness, but John could tell he was a bit wary of John's special relationship with the Sovereign Guard and its leader. Jacobs always worried that the regular military forces would be subservient to the Sovereign Guard in times of crisis. Hinkins was aware of this tension and relished it, as well as his role as the Sovereign's elite headmaster.

John ordered all Cabinet members to move their living quarters to the Sovereignty Building. They were to live, work, eat, and sleep there until the crisis had passed. In addition, John declared Sovereign's Law under Newland's constitution. Newland was under the strictest, tightest controls it had ever experienced in its seven-year tenure. Members of the legislature called in a frenzy, wondering what to do in light of the pending circumstances. They were directed to remain positive and calm and to spend time reassuring their constituents that Newland would endure this difficult situation. Patriotism gripped the nation in its time of need. Fortunately, Glitz had laid a solid foundation in seven years and built a national message upon it.

In less than a day, the entire state apparatus of Newland was committed to warding off the CBA menace. If only the Ideal State knew what exactly the threat was. Newland could only prepare and wait for the CBA to make its next move. John labeled the action against the CBA "Operation Bashed."

On day three of the Operation, Al Grudger arrived at the Sovereignty Building unannounced. Despite the rigid controls of Sovereign Law, he was allowed to enter and visit with John. Al shook John's hand and said, "Sovereign, good to see you. Glad we can talk."

John was taken aback by Al's unnatural formal tone. He replied, "Al, are you alright? It's just 'John' to you."

Al remained formal in tone and addressed his longtime acquaintance. "Sovereign, I cannot imagine what you are going through with this whole thing. I waited a while to visit. I wanted to give you time to adjust."

Still perturbed at Al's formality, John spoke more directly, "Can you help us? Help me?"

Al grew pale at John's request and replied tentatively, "Sovereign, I am unsure."

John abruptly interrupted him, "Damn it, Al. It's John; it's always been Al and John."

Al, realizing his inept formal tone, apologized. "Sorry, *John*," he emphasized. "It's been so chaotic the last few days. I wanted to see you before I left. I'm going."

"Going where?"

Al, the blushing billionaire, looked down as he spoke. "Probably the States. I don't know yet, but I must go. I'm leaving Newland."

John protested Al's decision vehemently. He tried desperately to dissuade him. "I need you now! Newland is threatened and needs every asset we can muster against the CBA. I was probably too direct with them and escalated the conflict, but they left me no choice. I need your talents. Our markets have slumped, and perception is not favorable to us. You owe it to me and to Newland to stay!"

Al became more ashen, trending toward overt sickness. Aligning with Al had always been Al's forte, and playing to his strength was no longer a positive attribute but a necessary reality. Al replied, "You've enraged them. They are going to destroy this place. The CBA is deep, relentless, and unyielding. You mishandled the meeting horribly. Now, your public display of exposing them was fatal to the relationship. It's over, John. All I can advise is to attempt to salvage some form of peace, a surrender that earns you a little something."

John was at a loss for words, actions, or thoughts for a while. A blend of anger, surprise, and disappointment, tempered with fear, gripped him. After a few moments, his ability to think returned, despite the fact his ability to reason had been battered by the emotional onslaught he was experiencing. "I asked you, who are they? Who or what is the CBA?"

Al, in his parting comments to his most lucrative client ever, replied, "I still don't know. Sam never knew, either. They just showed up with practically unlimited resources and hired us. All I can tell you is that they are powerful internationally, and they have permanently turned against you. It's hopeless."

John attempted to grapple with his current circumstances. With a sigh, he finally said, "Al, I can see that you are done. Done here, done with me, done with Newland. Anything more you can advise?"

Al thought briefly and responded, "I can only surmise that their next move won't be civil or gentle in any way. John, for what it's worth, I do wish you well. Now, I must go."

Al shook John's hand and left the office, vanishing from Newland like a parting foul wind.

CHAPTER 32

Newland Under Siege

One week after the less-than-glorious seven-year anniversary, Newland was in full defense mode. At no time in its existence had the young country ever experienced such a total onslaught of peril. The mood among Cabinet officials remained surprisingly positive, given the predictions of potential impending doom. Despite the drop in value of all of its business exchanges, the cash reserve infusions bolstered Newland's markets. The precipitous drop in prices had, for the time being, been stemmed by Newland's strategy to combat uncontrolled sell-offs. Newland had the financial reserves to apply to this situation, so it became a matter of where and when to utilize these resources. Jones, the Minister of Commerce, micromanaged the market portfolio as expertly as he could, given the seemingly formless yet formidable foe the nation faced.

On noon of the fifth day, in apparent contradiction to the thirty-day policy mentioned by the CBA, the unthinkable happened. Newland came under the effects of a relentless cyber-attack, which swept across the nation like an uncontrollable plague. Banks, businesses, and government entities were immediately compromised. Every aspect of Newland's existence was under siege, including its military. John was kept up to date as a flurry of bad news poured into the Sovereignty Building.

The worst aspects of this scenario were playing out, as John and Newland had no plan in place to deal with a cyber-attack of this proportion. The CBA had made its first move, a cyber salvo, which proved devastatingly effective.

Reports of people storming the banks, stores, and the square in front of the Sovereignty Building were mounting within minutes. Glitz urged John to address the people immediately via a backup manual radio system. Printing presses were churning out leaflets to inform Newlanders of the attack. John took to the airwaves and urged people to remain calm and resolved to defeat the CBA menace, which the Sovereign railed against in his desperate oratory.

As chaos continued to abound, the situation in Newland grew worse. The power grid was jammed beyond repair, and hence, electricity was cut off to all of Newland proper. Surprisingly, Imploria was still functioning in terms of power due to its antiquated electric grid and archaic delivery system, which had yet to be modernized in its reconstruction. Imploria's computers and other apparatuses, which had been modernized, were compromised and shut down.

As John and his Cabinet waded through the communications and logistics nightmare, they employed manual means to address the crisis. The results were sporadic at best. John called for his car and asked to view the situation on the ground first-hand. The Sovereign Guard immediately complied. Hinkins was alarmed and personally brought an armored carrier to escort his Sovereign across a devastated Newland. He drove the vehicle with the assistance of two of his best officers.

John watched in horror as the ordinarily safe and serene streets of Newland were transformed into avenues of discontent, cluttered with worried and panicking citizens. Banks were closed, store shelves had been emptied, and Glitz informed John that uncontrolled radio broadcasts were dominating Newland's airwaves, blaming John and his government for Newland's woes.

The communications barrage launched by the CBA was massive. Newland's poster displays and primitive flyers on the streets urging patience and patriotism proved to be no match for the onslaught of the CBA information blitz. As John visited a supermarket, he noticed the barren shelves where abundance flourished a few days earlier. He took umbrage in the fact that, despite the chaos, there had been no looting in Newland. Newlanders paid cash for every item they could locate amidst the overwhelming demand in the stores. A beleaguered manager approached John in total distress and asked his Sovereign for an explanation. "Sovereign, what is going on? This is awful. We are being told you are to blame. Surely this is untrue, sir."

In an attempt to calm one citizen among the thousands in distress, John addressed the rattled retailer. "What is your name?"

"Bing, sir," the manager replied.

"Bing, I assure you that this attack is not my fault. It is coming from bad people, people we don't understand. We must all stand strong for Newland now. Our country's survival depends on it."

Bing continued honestly despite the leers of the Sovereign Guards, "Sovereign, radio reports are not only blaming you but say that the attacks will cease if you go—if you leave. This message is spreading all across Newland. My cousin on the north end of Newland manages a similar store to mine, and he has received the same message."

John was speechless as the magnitude of the CBA attack overwhelmed him.

Hinkins, witnessing the entire conversation, said, "Bing, you are a successful businessman, where is your loyalty to our Sovereign? He has provided us with everything. I expect nothing but unfettered loyalty from you and our citizens. Fight for our homeland; fight for our Sovereign."

Bing looked at the Sovereign's guardian and spoke softly to the general, "Sir, I am a quiet and peaceful man. I am not political, not fancy, just a hard-working Newlander. Look at what has happened in less than two days. It is utter chaos."

John nodded at Hinkins, ready to depart from this venue of veritable vacancy.

Hinkins, in a parting word, shouted, "Be loyal, Bing. Be loyal." The manager stood silent among his empty shelves and watched them go.

The effects of the relentless barrage against Newland continued. People began to flee the nation, as the airports were flooded with flyers seeking other destinations. Newland's Transportation Minister, Rhoda, contacted John via manual radio. "Sir," she said over the crackling radio signal, "the planes are leaving one after the other, full of passengers. They are empty upon return. It's an evacuation, Sovereign. What shall I do?"

John inquired, "How are the planes taking off and landing without tower assistance?"

Rhoda responded, "Sovereign, people show up, pay cash, and the planes come and go without tower assistance. Our towers are not operational, but the planes still fly."

Rhoda had been among Newland's most effective Cabinet members. She had emigrated from South Africa and presided over an infrastructure boom never experienced by a nation Newland's size. In a sense, Rhoda was pleased to see her state-of-the-art airport operate so efficiently, even without the aid of computers.

John, in an abrupt tone, said, "Let them go. Do not stop them. If they wish to abandon us, so be it."

Rhoda could sense her Sovereign's frustration. "Sir, there will be a day when people fly in here again. I will stay with you, Sovereign, and assist you until that day arrives."

John thanked her and signed off.

As the days of crisis persisted, all sectors, including the stock markets, schools, and businesses, remained closed or severely impaired. The citizens remained nonviolent but took to the streets, wandering about in a desperate search for answers. The impacts of the CBA's actions were taking a severe toll on Newland.

At the Sovereignty Building, minister after minister convened, strategized, and pleaded with one another for solutions. To date, there were none. Food was also beginning to dwindle, even among the Newland elite. John had not been home or even had the opportunity to check on Mary and his sons. Sovereign Guards peacefully surrounded his home to protect Newland's First Family.

To either Newland's credit or John's, there had been no reported violence, major acts of dissidence, or theft among the populace.

Finally, after five days of relentless cyber-attacks, the bombardment ceased, and systems were restored. Messages were thrust upon every computer screen that another all-out attack would occur in one week unless John left the country. As the nation reinstated its computer networks, the sense of cyber siege was everywhere. Newland's technology sector was still dependent on the CBA's whim or will. John felt helpless, as did his Cabinet. The communications war against the Sovereign, however, did not cease; in fact, it increased with each passing day.

On the third day after computer access was restored, the CBA began sending harsher messaging. Broadcasting from as many media sources as the CBA could muster, they informed Newlanders that "John A. Kinley, dictator of Newland, must depart by the given date, or the cyber-attacks, along with other attacks, will be launched. This time, without cease or abatement." The final message from the CBA was direct and to the point. "Act now to save yourselves and your nation and avoid the immeasurable harm that will occur if Kinley remains."

Exhausted from lack of sleep and pervasive stress, John asked his Sovereign Guard to drive him to his home to see Mary and their sons. Upon arrival, he hugged her and exclaimed, "It's the CBA! They are all in to oust me. I have less than a week to decide whether to stay or go."

Mary was nervous. She trembled in a manner John had never experienced before. She spoke briefly, "John, I'm scared— for the boys and me. Please make a decision, do something. Help us."

"I will, but I must go now. Time has also become a foe in this battle against the CBA." He kissed her and left, a slight weight lifted from his shoulders after seeing his family safe, though shaken.

He returned to the Sovereignty Building without delay. Upon his arrival, he observed the crowds that had gathered in the large front square of the Sovereignty Building. After witnessing the gathering, John summoned his Cabinet. Though tired and fearful, they remained loyal. Newland's brain trust was frayed, but willing to listen and aid their Sovereign. Unfortunately, there were sincere doubts about the population at large, as Glitz had been out-maneuvered and overrun by the CBA's information campaign, which dwarfed his efforts.

John addressed his Cabinet in a tone of despair they had never heard from their all-powerful Sovereign. "My loyal Newlanders, we have been under siege and attack. Our citizens have, by and large, remained faithful, peaceful, and committed to our causes. They are law-abiding, even in the face of danger. Time is of the essence. I am to leave in three days, or the CBA will launch an attack with more fervor than their previous blitz. I believe they are more than capable of doing this. I have reached out, to no avail, for international assistance from the United Nations. In this fight, sadly, we stand alone. Outside of our beloved Capitol Building, crowds of our citizens are gathering. They want answers and solutions, but I am fearful. Their numbers are mounting daily. They do not deserve the prospect of destruction. I ask all of you to assist me with a solution to our problems. You, as a group, have been loyal, competent public servants. Now, I need—we need—extraordinary ideas and actions to save our nation. The rest of the world has abandoned us in our hour of need. I don't know if I should stay or go."

Hinkins urged, "Sovereign, you must stay. These cyber barbarians will attempt to destroy us whether you stay or go."

John addressed his most loyal follower, "Hinkins, they are far more than cyber barbarians. They could use capital, propaganda, and even military might if necessary. We have, perhaps, just seen the beginning of their arsenal."

Hinkins replied, "All the more reason to stand and fight now, Sovereign. They will turn Newland into a serfdom."

John looked across the table at his entire Cabinet. He inquired, "Any ideas?"

There was silence.

"Any thoughts?"

Still silence.

Finally, Jones, the Minister of Commerce, felt compelled to offer something. He told the group, "We have reserves, cash, gold, other gems. If they attack again, we can use these resources to survive."

John inquired, "But for how long?"

Jones offered an estimate, "Sovereign, perhaps a few weeks. I am unsure. If people continue to flee, if we cannot trade with our neighbors, then we are doomed. International trade is the lifeblood of any nation. If they apply an international tourniquet to us, we could be at subsistence levels in weeks."

Nap Davis, the Foreign Minister, spoke up at this dire prediction. "Sovereign, surely, with all of our deals and diplomacy, we can find a wealthy nation to float us."

John spoke to his Cabinet again, realizing he had to be the source of strength and optimism at a time when he sorely needed to be the recipient of both. "My loyal Cabinet, I wish benevolence was a universal attribute. I'm afraid the world is watching the CBA invade our land. They may fear a similar fate, who knows? Newland was a good investment, a solid, stable deal. That is no longer the case."

Every minister was emotionally united with their Sovereign leader. Never had there been a moment in the history of Newland where every ounce of the leadership's energy had been more focused on its absolute ruler. John knew this; he sensed this and spoke further. "My friends, I will leave you now. It's about five p.m. We will reconvene at ten. You have five hours to come up with a plan, or I will. Now, I must address the masses from our balcony."

Glitz intervened, "Sovereign, the world press corps is watching. What will you say? What is your plan?"

"The truth," John replied. "I will tell Newland and the world the absolute truth. Let the world spectate; the truth will not change. Out of truth, mercy and justice will ensue."

John walked to the large balcony of the Sovereignty Building. Countless times, he had brought good tidings to the masses of Newland. That night, he was the bearer of less-than-savory news. He stood alone, armed with a hand-held microphone. He looked across the large Sovereignty Square, packed to capacity with people. No signs, just people waiting for their leader to address them. He noticed the press cameras everywhere, reminiscent of earlier days when his fledgling nation had been birthed, grew, and prospered. Now, it seemed like an eternity since those glorious days of rancorous rallies. Thousands of people grew silent as John approached the balcony and began to address them.

John began, "My fellow countrymen, we are under attack by an evil group of wrongdoers who want to destroy us, our way of life, our values, everything."

A man shouted from the crowd, "Sovereign, save us!"

His plea was joined by others, at first individually and then with a chorus of chants. "Save us!"

John was visibly moved by the crowd's apparent faith in his ability to rescue them from the peril at hand. He continued, "I assure you that I will explore every remedy available to us. Ministers from every department are working on this around the clock, as am I. Please return to your homes. Stay united and help each other. I do not wish to belabor our predicament, but it is dire. If any nation so desires, please join us in our fight. Your assistance is requested. We need help in our hour of need. Our fate today may be your fate tomorrow. Let no nation fall prey to the tyranny to which we, in Newland, are being subjected. Please assist us."

The crowd was moved tremendously by their Sovereign's speech. They began to shout "Newland!" over and over again. Many cried; others began jumping up and down. The display was one of national unity, not national fear. John was consoled by this show of national pride. He left the balcony with a wave to his people and walked to his empty office.

At nine-thirty, a note arrived from his Cabinet. It read, "No solutions."

His ministers were at a loss. The solution was entirely in John's hands. John sat at his desk, motionless, head down, and thinking relentlessly. The phone rang on his personal Sovereign line. His number was available to a select group of Newlanders and foreign officials. He answered, and to his surprise, it was Carlene.

John spoke to her in a light but defenseless tone, "Oh, hello, Carlene. Rough times here. Are you in Imploria?"

Carlene was quick to respond. "Yes, I am, and it's not very good here either. Actually, it's a disaster. My hotel is running out of food. Oh, they have basics, but the steaks are gone, no champagne. It's horrible. John, do something!"

John tried to convince her of his plight. "I am under an ultimatum, a horrible threat. Please, let me work through this mess."

Carlene, merciless as usual, was direct in her response. "Fix this, fix this now! It's your mess. You fell for that CBA line of crap, and now they've trapped you."

John tried to reason with her. "I'm trying, really, I am. Do you have any ideas? Can you help me?"

Carlene lambasted him without hesitating. "Cut a deal. Do whatever you have to; just get something big for you and for me, too. Every day you wait, every moment you ponder your fate, you lose ground."

John began to argue hopelessly with the perennial object of his affection. "They won't deal. They just want me to go, or chaos will break loose in less than a week. Al has left us. I have so few people to turn to."

"Chaos has already broken loose; it's a way of life in your ideal state."

John inquired, "May I send a plane for you?"

"A plane for me? Absolutely not. The worst place to be right now is in Capitol City. If you blow it—the negotiations or whatever—and there's an invasion, riots, or something, I want none of it."

John knew his pleas were futile. He ceased his arguments and merely said, "Okay, I must go now. I meet with my Cabinet at ten."

Carlene, insisting on the final word, stated, "You created this mess, and you can fix it. Be a tyrant, not a theorist. Be the historical son of a bitch I always wanted you to be. This is no time for philosopher kings."

Feeling abandoned again, John told Carlene, "You sound like my wife, like my Mary—minus the tenderness, of course."

Carlene hung up the phone without further comment.

CHAPTER 33

A Visit from an Angel

John grew anxious as he waited for the meeting with his Cabinet. With no ideas and no solutions, hope was waning. A private of the Sovereign Guard knocked on his office door. Upon entering, he announced, "Sovereign, a young lady, sir, wishes to meet with you."

John replied tiredly, "Please, not now. I'm on the verge of one of the most important meetings of my life."

The young guard showed great resolve and exclaimed, "Sovereign, she insists she can help you! She's been waiting to see you for hours and refuses to leave."

Perplexed but intrigued by such a bold assertion, John ordered his guard to show her in. "Give her ten minutes, then come and remove her. Private, I've got dragons to slay, and you want me to be a babysitter."

The elite Private eagerly complied and brought the young girl into the Sovereign's office. The girl entered quietly. She appeared to be about eighteen with blonde hair and a petite frame. She was ghostly pale, and John felt an instant wave of awkwardness in her presence.

"Sovereign, my name is Angel," she introduced herself.

John noticed a distinct brogue. "What are you—Irish, Scottish, Welsh?" he asked.

The young girl replied, "Of sorts, but today, I am a Newlander."

"Young lady, I appreciate your willingness to help, but I'm in a tight spot. The fate of our beloved Newland rests upon me now. I can give you ten minutes for your good heart and loyalty," John told her rather directly.

Angel, in light of her position, asserted her thoughts. She spoke without fear or hesitation. "Sovereign, since I have only ten minutes, allow me the floor."

Impressed by her tender, John sat back. "The floor is yours, young lady. Proceed."

In a voice slightly higher than a whisper, Angel said, "Sovereign, I can help you to defeat this CBA foe."

John looked up with a humored grin but then saw her resolve. She was serious. He replied, "Well, you're the first. Continue."

In the same tone, she said, "I know something about computers and other things."

"Where did you attend school?" John asked curiously.

"I was homeschooled, Sovereign. I have no formal degrees." Looking directly into his eyes, she persisted, "I think I know how they attacked us. With a little time, I believe I can find out where their attack came from."

John was intrigued by everything about his ten-minute guest, from her appearance to her demeanor to her offers of assistance. He responded, "Little time, my dear Angel, is exactly what we have. Surely, you would not jest with your Sovereign."

Angel responded, "Rest assured, sir, I would never jest or dishonor my Sovereign. Allow me to meet with your Minister of Science and Technology, Yates, I believe?"

John replied, "Yes, it's Yates, very good. I'm impressed." John assessed her and then continued, "Yates is sharp and very talented. He studied at the very best—both MIT and Stanford. He ensured that our hardware and software were impeccable—" He paused, adding, "Until now."

The ten-minute mark arrived, and the Sovereign Guard reentered the room. He very carefully addressed his Sovereign and the intriguing guest, saying, "Sovereign, I believe it's time, sir."

John was pleased with the Private's obedience and praised him. "Yes, Private, it is time. You have done well in your service to Newland. You brought me this young lady, Angel, and have followed my orders meticulously. I order you to take her to Minister Yates; he's in the building. If anyone questions your authority, even superiors, tell them you are acting on my orders. Until further notice, you are assigned to Angel. See to her needs." John turned to Angel and said, "Thank you for your assistance. I fear the problem is far more than cyber, but we have little in the way of cyber defense or cyber-attack ability. Do your best."

As she hovered by the door, John couldn't help but think that there was something about her that made her seem innately trustworthy, though he wasn't convinced of the young woman's abilities. His despair lingered, but he managed to inquire of his visitor some further questions. "How much time do you need, and what will this cost Newland? What is your price?"

Angel responded, "Give me a day, maybe two at the most. I am a volunteer, Sovereign, no price for now. I only ask that my assistance be kept secret between you, me, Yates, and the

Private. I want no leaks, gaffes, or loose lips alerting these foes of our moves."

"Done!" John exclaimed. He admonished her only once, "Angel, I don't know what you can do, but do it quickly. Incidentally, have you any ideas for confronting any future attacks they may launch?"

Seizing on his admonition, she daintily apprised him, "Yes, I do, Sovereign. Be prepared to act immediately upon my advice, sir."

John was amazed by her confidence asserted with no trace of arrogance or hubris. "I shall," he said. "I am ready." The two young people departed John's office in search of Yates. John, for the first time in days, hung on to a glimmer of hope in his optimistic constitution.

The next morning, John received word from Yates that a young woman escorted by a young Sovereign Guard had approached him on John's orders. Over the radio, Yates told John that the trio had worked all night at the Technology Ministry in search of a solution.

Hopeful, John inquired, "Yates, is she for real?"

Not used to a colloquial Sovereign, Yates replied, "Yes, Sovereign. She's for real, as you phrase it, and different. She knows what she is doing, almost instinctively, sir." He went further, explaining, "I detect phonies in this business every day; they're easy to spot, but she is good—extremely good."

John summoned Hinkins, head of his Sovereign Guard, and traveled to the Technology Ministry wing of the Sovereignty Building. Upon entering, Angel was sitting in a chair behind a computer, working furiously. Yates stood behind her, more solicitous than demanding and watching her every move. Her

Sovereign Guard stood silent and attentive behind them both. John burst into the room, asking, "Angel, how is it going?"

Before she could answer, Yates declared, "Sovereign, she is amazing! She hasn't left to eat or drink; she works non-stop. She's the best I've ever seen."

Angel gently smiled and continued working. Hinkins' presence caused the Private to stand erect at attention without comment. John looked at Hinkins, hoping he would place his Private at ease, but he was focused on Angel and Yates. Hinkins finally realized he had a subordinate present and replied, "Private, at ease. Why are you here? Who ordered this? I don't know you. What's your name?"

John interrupted before the youthful guard could respond, "Hinkins, this fine young Private brought us Angel on his good judgment. I asked him to remain with us throughout this ordeal. It's all on me."

Hinkins, stern as usual, refused to comment other than telling his Private, "So ordered."

"Yes, sir," said the Private.

Angel looked up after about fifteen more minutes. To everyone's surprise, she quietly announced, "I found them, Sovereign. I know where they are centrally located."

An immediate sense of inquisitive amazement gripped the room as those present awaited her discovery. She continued, "Looks like a base cell in New York City, with connecting cells worldwide. My preliminary findings indicate a center base with feeders."

John was almost speechless at this announcement. He was dumbstruck and dazed by this information. Finally, he managed to speak, "How do you know this? Are you sure?"

Angel looked up at him from her chair and stated, "I broke their code, sir. It was complex—about the best I've seen—but I deciphered it. The process took me a bit longer than usual. I've been running checks to be sure, but now, I'm positive."

John inquired immediately, "What shall we do? How do we proceed?"

Angel said, "I've been thinking about this for hours. I have a plan that may work." All eyes and ears awaited her next words. She proceeded, "Sovereign, let's use Newland's unique code to send out a covert message that you are leaving in a day."

Yates interrupted, "In our code? They'll never understand it."

Angel looked at John and blandly stated, "Your code, Newland's code, was so easy to break. It took less than an hour."

John looked over at Yates, who sat silently as his work was disrobed. Angel continued, "Rest assured, Sovereign, they know your code, probably deciphered it years ago."

In a mild rebuke of Yates, John stated, "Yates, you assured me years ago that our code, your unique invention, could not be broken."

Yates hurriedly sat down at the computer, hastily typed something, and sat back. He pointed at the inscription and looked over at Angel, challenging her to react. Angel went to the screen, pushed a few buttons, and responded to Yates in front of everyone, "Minister Yates, happy birthday to you, sir."

Yates sat back in quiet disbelief, shaking his head, and exclaimed, "She's got it! I don't know how, but she does."

With Angel's credibility established beyond reproach, the conversation moved to the plan of action. John queried, "Why the false message of my early departure?"

Angel responded, "Maybe, just maybe, when they think they have won, they will focus on their easy takeover of Newland. It will be a taking of the cyberbait of sorts. If they do that, sir, I'll make sure it's cyber poison."

Yates was still reeling in astonishment. "How?"

Angel replied, "No time to explain that now; trust me on this, for if they don't take the bait, we will have to change course quickly."

John pounded on the desk, exclaiming, "Do it! Place my departure at noon tomorrow in the code. Mark it 'top secret' and send it."

Angel and Yates sat down at the computer and typed the message. They all watched as Angel hit the send button, and the screen broadcasted the message. Angel stood, looked directly at Hinkins, and said, "Please, hide him somewhere. A bunker, maybe, or anywhere close but confidential. We cannot afford a breach in security now. If we are to succeed, the entire world must think the Sovereign has left Newland."

John stood up without hesitation and told Hinkins, "Let's go." He then walked over to Angel, thanked her, and offered, "I'll send you food, provisions, and necessities, just ask. You are welcome to stay with us in my underground safe house or to remain here."

Angel did not respond to the Sovereign's offer; she merely inquired about the readiness of Newland's military and was assured that the entire nation was still under Sovereign Law. John left for his palatial bunker with Hinkins while Angel, her Private, and Yates stayed in the Technology Ministry.

CHAPTER 34

The CBA Takes the Bait

John arrived at his underground safe house under the cloak of secrecy. Mary and the boys were already there. Hinkins joined them as their only security. They could not risk anyone witnessing or sharing that John was still in Newland. Within two hours, Angel called John on his Sovereign line. It was archaic, so antiquated that it was extremely secure.

Angel informed him, "Sovereign, they took the bait. Messages throughout their system are celebrating, in fact."

John, unconvinced, pressed her, "Are you sure, absolutely sure?"

"Positive, sir."

"Where is Yates?"

Angel replied, "Asleep, sir. He worked hours with no rest. Sleep is advisable, as I may need him in the coming hours."

John replied, "Fine, let him rest. What do you think I should do now?"

"Sovereign, I will offer a solution, but you must authorize the action. We can go big, if you wish, or play defense. I suggest we try to take them down in light of their actions toward Newland. They made a huge mistake in ceasing their cyber-attack. They had us. They broke into our systems with relative ease. No question. Could have and should have finished us off," Angel reasoned, pausing to hear John's reply.

John was listening intently and merely said, "Please continue, I want to know my options and your thoughts. I fully understand the predicament."

Angel offered her thoughts. "I can draft a new code, a virus of sorts, exclusively for Newland. I can deter any new attack they may launch and then go on offense."

"What type of offense?" John inquired.

Angel did not pause, "All out cyber war, sir. I can freeze all of their assets and international holdings and, ultimately, transfer the wealth to Newland."

John was beyond belief in his young cyber master's confidence. He replied, "Surely, this is far too ambitious to succeed. The CBA must be better prepared to deal with such an onslaught. This seems like piracy to me."

Angel was relentless in her response despite maintaining her ultra-whisper tone. "Sir, while I was waiting to see if they would fall into our trap, I checked their resources. They have military might, including planes, tanks, ships, and, sadly, nuclear capability. I even found a cache of mercenary resources to supplement their arsenal."

John interrupted, "Please, I've had my fill of mercenaries to last a lifetime." Then, he paused to allow her to continue.

Angel did. "Sir, the CBA is going to strike at Newland again. They think you have gone, so they will move forward with whatever their next move may be."

John was still unsure of himself and still wary of Angel's abilities. He inquired further, "How much time do I have to decide?"

Angel warned him, "Sir, the sooner the better. Their system is wide open. If it were to close, I'd have to figure out how to break in again."

John took a deep breath, sighed, and said, "Do it." Then, he inquired, "What are our capabilities now? Are we at full capacity?"

"Yes," Angel assured him. "The CBA has not reignited their attack, especially since they believe you have left Newland. We are at full technological capacity and operating fine."

A weight lifted from John's shoulders. "And what about new attacks? If the CBA were to attack anew, could you stop them?"

Angel paused. "Well, I cannot be sure until the nature of the attack is revealed."

John appreciated her honesty but was left in a quandary about Newland's defenses. Sensing his anxiety, Angel told him, "Sir, worry not about your defense; you are on offense now."

He acquiesced to her characterization of the situation and asked her to move forward.

John was in hiding from the world. Even though the CBA was convinced he had departed his beloved Newland, others were in a quandary. The press, the citizens of Newland, and even John's Cabinet were all asking the same question. Where was the Sovereign of the Ideal State? John read the reports and became antsy. He ordered Hinkins to keep the Cabinet and military on full alert in his absence. They obeyed, even though they, too, wondered who was governing Newland and for how long.

The national mood was tense. Many Newlanders had left the country; others who remained were concerned about their nation's fate.

Angel called John to inform him that the "poison bait" had been put in place and was set to launch at 11:00 a.m. the next day. John resigned himself to wait. He asked Hinkins to have Nap Davis, the Foreign Minister, reach out to the international community for assistance. John had secretly hoped that some nations would assist Newland in its dire time of need, but they did not. He took solace in the fact that the CBA would probably see the move as further proof that the desperate nation without its leader needed help. It would, at a minimum, confirm their belief that John was gone.

As the seconds ticked closer to eleven o'clock, Angel sat watching her computer in a vigil to her skills. Yates, awake, alert, and more curious than jealous, was also watching with tenacity. John waited in his underground fortress with Hinkins. The clock struck 11:00 a.m.

There was silence at the Technology Ministry and silence in the bunker as the vast majority of Newlanders sat in oblivion, unaware of what may or may not transpire. Angel punched computer key after computer key as a conductor in a cyber symphony awaiting a crescendo. After a half hour of activity, she raised her head from her computer perch and spoke to Yates. "It's done. Success."

In a state of disbelief, Yates asked her, "What shall I do now?"

Angel instructed the Technology Minister, "Inform the Sovereign at once. I cannot control what will happen next. He must lead us through the CBA's reaction. They may or may not be aware that we have seized their assets and now control their operating systems. Their manual response, if any, is unpredictable. I know not if my move was check or checkmate."

Yates phoned John immediately after the briefing from Angel. John asked to speak with Angel at once and questioned her about her findings. "Angel, thank you. I need facts now, absolute facts; please qualify anything that is not factual as conjecture or otherwise. I understand that you have attained success?"

Angel replied, "Yes, sir, this is what I can tell you for sure: We were successful in all aspects of our counter-hack. The National Bank of Newland now has close to ten trillion dollars in its secured treasury account. We have their monetary assets. They know they are gone but may not know how or where. It should be obvious."

John asked further, "Who are they?"

"This is conjecture, sir. They are a broken and confused foe with a physical base in Brazil, somewhere in the rainforest. More conjecture, sir, is that I believe they will counterattack soon; however, I don't know the details."

John was too apprehensive to be elated at this apparent victory. He emerged from his bunker and headed to the Sovereignty Building. Strict orders were given not to discuss the move and success against the CBA. John ordered Hinkins to prepare his special forces in the Sovereign Guard, the New Berets, for a physical attack on the CBA headquarters in Brazil. He was prepared to risk violating Brazilian air space and possibly international law. His desire was a surprise strike at the CBA at its core location. Angel continued to monitor the CBA activity as the elusive foe's computer gurus attempted to deal with the reality of the unthinkable event that had befallen them. Angel reported cyber chaos in their futile attempts to restore their lost wealth.

International reports began to leak, reporting that the Sovereign was still, in fact, in Newland and still in power. Nonetheless, John decided to maintain his presence in the Sovereignty Building.

Hinkins briefed John after consulting with Angel. Her data suggested the existence of a dark and austere complex deep in the Brazilian jungle guarded by an elite mercenary force. Hinkins reported that he had one hundred New Berets ready to pounce on the CBA at the Sovereign's order. John questioned Hinkins' deployment of only one hundred New Berets; he wanted to utilize more of his elite special forces. Hinkins assured him that if engaged, one hundred would prove sufficient.

CHAPTER 35

New Berets on Jungle Duty

John's deadline to leave Newland had come and gone, and Newland had an additional ten trillion dollars in its national coffers, yet the nation was still unsure of what was transpiring inside and outside of the Ideal State. The CBA did not take any retaliatory action toward Newland the day following the impressive cyber coup. This may have been due to a lack of ability or a lack of realization of what had happened to them. Either way, John was determined to strike and strike hard at his ever-present nemesis.

Another bright sunny day greeted Newland and its capital city. John arose from his couch in the Sovereignty Office, showered, and called Hinkins. He gave the order to strike the CBA facility in Brazil. Hinkins, in turn, called his New Beret commander, Cain, and commenced the action. One hundred New Berets flew toward their target in the Brazilian jungle. John was hopeful the element of surprise and lethal force would bring him a quick and total victory.

Newland's special forces parachuted undetected near the compound in the Brazilian jungle. The New Berets attacked the CBA compound with fierce firepower, blasting through the elite mercenary defenses with speed and surprise. The CBA leadership team inside of the main building scrambled to remedy what they deemed a computer glitch in their system. They had not yet realized the magnitude of the attack or its results. The transfer of assets from their accounts had not yet fully registered with them.

The inner circle of CBA leadership, including Combs, Burns, and Amos, were oblivious to the impending military action until the Newland force came crashing through the compound. At that point, they decided to congregate in the complex's main control center and attempt to defend their core facility.

In the meantime, the CBA mercenary force was overwhelmed and crushed. The castle-like complex was riddled with bullets and explosives. Hinkins gave Cain the strictest orders to take no prisoners on this mission. The CBA force for hire saw their ranks dwindle, though the New Berets's causalities were minimal.

As Cain burst into the main center of the CBA complex, a stunned and horrified trio of Combs, Burns, and Amos, along with their minions, attempted to thwart the Newland barrage. They returned fire as Newland's elite Berets stormed into the room.

Cain was shot in the head and killed immediately.

Both sides continued the battle with tremendous firepower. Burns and Amos were shot dead in a flurry of bullets. Combs rushed to a red control button on the computer dais. He successfully pushed it but was riddled with bullets in the process and fell dead on the spot.

After only fifteen minutes of internal fighting, all of the CBA members inside the complex, their security forces, and other personnel lay dead. Approximately five hundred CBA members and their associates had perished. Twenty-five New Berets were dead, with another fifteen wounded. At the cessation of hostilities, the remaining New Berets began to assess the damage, lamenting that their commander, Cain, was dead.

A terrible rumbling began, shaking the room.

"It was the red button!" shouted a soldier.

The New Berets made a sudden dash for the door. As they ran for the exits of the main facility, buildings exploded one after the other. The elite attackers were in full stride, attempting to exit the jungle inferno brought on by a desperate last attempt to defray an abrupt and overwhelming defeat. As New Berets fell due to the destructive blasts, one final and large explosion rendered the entire area a huge crater. The battle was over; the jungle was silent. The CBA's core was no more. A large hole loomed quietly in an immense and desolate forest on the cusp of a dark Brazilian night. Only a handful of New Berets managed to clear the blast zone in time, limping their way to two scouts who remained on the outskirts of the battle. They'd observed the carnage and reported the results to their Sovereign.

CHAPTER 36

Newland Rises

John received the news of the battle in Brazil with mixed emotions. He was saddened by the loss of nearly one hundred of his finest, most loyal soldiers but pleased with the success of the total destruction of the CBA headquarters and their leadership. Angel continued to monitor the computer activity of the CBA up to and after the self-destruction button was pushed. She informed John and Yates that activity was still occurring on behalf of the CBA in the cyber realm despite the apparent destruction of their headquarters.

"What does this mean?" John inquired of his young acquaintance when they met for the final time in John's office in the Sovereignty Building.

Angel responded, "This means they are elsewhere, elusive and evasive. Something or someone may have survived."

John replied promptly, "But they are broke, militarily grounded, and leaderless, right?"

Angel replied, "Yes, sir, at least, as you might say, 'on paper.' Or, as I would say, 'on computer.' The destruction button was manual—a backup. I couldn't stop the detonation. That may have been happenstance, or perhaps it was planned. Only time will tell what remains of the CBA."

Angel rose from her chair with a floating ease. She told John and Hinkins, "I am done here. I must go now."

John decried, "You are a national hero! I want to honor you and make a statement for the ages. You saved Newland."

Angel walked over to where John was standing and placed her delicate hand on John's shoulder. He had never felt such a gentle wisp fall upon him as she addressed him. "Sir, be on guard. The CBA is dangerous."

He interrupted, "You mean *was* dangerous?"

"No, sir. *Is*," she insisted. "Newland is safe for now, but their kind has been around for ages. Beware."

John was puzzled by the young woman's innate knowledge of the CBA. He inquired, "How do you know so much about the CBA? You learned so much from their code?"

She replied in a somber, gentle tone, "In a way, sir, I have known their code long before computers." With that, she stopped herself from explaining further.

John insisted, "Please, tell us more."

Angel merely told them one final time, "I am done here, and I'll be in touch soon."

John protested, "Soon? I'm about to proclaim what has just transpired to all of Newland. This is nothing short of a miracle, and you deserve public acclaim for your efforts."

John sensed his accolades for Angel were not convincing his young heroine, so he persisted. "Think of how proud your parents will be. I'll award you Newland's highest medal, the Order of Truth, and construct a monument to you, or how about naming our new national park after you?" John was beaming with pride and delight as the young lady remained staid and composed.

She maintained her dainty but steady whisper tone and replied, "Sovereign, there is one thing I would appreciate."

Without hesitation, John said, "Name it."

She looked at Newland's leader in the presence of Hinkins and several Cabinet members who had joined them and said, "Free Imploria, sir. Give them back their independence."

As gasps erupted around the room, all eyes turned to the Sovereign. John was startled but said, "Free Imploria? Why?" Before she could respond, he felt compelled to continue, "Angel, we've spent millions on that island. It's a success, and the people are happy to be Newlanders. Imploria is part of our national fabric; they are one with us."

Angel paused before saying, "Newland has always been a place of truth, honor, and justice, but sir, what we did in Imploria was wrong—carnage, greed, and horror. Let us live and prosper in Newland as a beacon to these ideals. Sir, you are a just man; display that trait to the world. By the way, sir, on the balance sheet, I believe the ten trillion dollars or so we just received in our treasury will more than offset a few million lost in Imploria."

John winced as he listened to his young miracle worker's sharp but honest criticism.

Mary, who was present, looked over at John and nodded with approval as others awaited their Sovereign's decision. Angel grew silent after her request.

Finally, John addressed her, "Angel, consider it done. Imploria shall be offered its independence. Of course, if they desire to remain with us, we should accommodate our neighbors."

Angel looked up at John and said, "Make the offer, sir."

John nodded. "Understood."

As she prepared to leave their presence, Angel stopped and spoke again. "Before I depart, Sovereign, there is another matter."

"Oh," John replied. "Perhaps something for you?"

"Oh no, sir. Something exclusively for you. Issue an order exiling Carlene from Newland, once and for all."

Equally as astonished by this request as her first, John proclaimed, "So ordered." His cheeks flushed with embarrassment.

"Thank you, Mr. Kinley," she said. "Rule wisely, justly, and firmly. I wish you and Newland the very best." She departed with the young Sovereign Guard private at her side.

One week later, Imploria graciously accepted Newland's offer of independence. They immediately offered a trade and peace treaty with Newland and authored a press release urging other nations to do the same. Carlene was served an order of exile the day before its independence was declared. She was served the papers at the pool in the Carlene Hotel. As she was escorted to the airport and flown back to the United States, she was reported to have demanded a phone call to the Sovereign. None was granted, but she vowed to someday return with a vengeance toward all. Her assets had also been frozen in Newland and were summarily turned over to Imploria with its independence and full restoration of its assets.

Within the first week of its independence, Imploria's governor rededicated its magnificent hotel. It seemed someone had informed the governor, soon-to-be president, that a particular young lady had inspired an omnipotent leader to give Imploria its sovereignty back. The Carlene Hotel was aptly renamed "The Angel."

Within one week of the renaming, a mysterious but beautiful white flower bloomed in front of the Angel in a glorious garden. Botanists could not determine the exact nature of the species, but experts believed it to be an extinct crocus variety referenced in antiquity.

In Newland, the Cabinet and John were very subdued about the newfound trillions in their coffers. Yates was instructed in his capacity as Technology Minister to secure and protect all funds in concert with Jones, the Minister of Commerce, who would invest and decipher the multiple currencies now in Newland's possession. Manual deposits of currency and precious metals were ordered to be stored in a central vault to ensure access to actual resources in the event of any attempts to raid Newland's treasury with a cyber-attack.

John issued a proclamation creating a permanent state of exile for those who fled Newland during its recent crisis. The proclamation provided exceptions for those who could unequivocally prove planned travel, travel for health or family reasons with an open-ended exception to be decided by officers of Newland. Polygraphs were to be mandatory in any such application. In John's steadfast view, the truth would determine the loyalty of those who legitimately deserved to be citizens of Newland. The assets of those who fled were frozen and placed in the same account as the usurped CBA funds. In his view, those who abandoned Newland in its time of dire need were no better than the CBA and its minions who attempted to destroy it.

The entire nation, from its Cabinet to its legislature, was in full restoration mode after the CBA onslaught. Victory over the CBA was carefully but truthfully disseminated by Glitz and his

Information Ministry to an interested and eager nation determined to find out what exactly had occurred to bring their beloved nation back from the brink of extinction. The facts that had been made public were true, but most of the details remained sealed within the intelligence community and a select group of Newland's governing class. For most, the cessation of hostilities and almost immediate return of progress to the Ideal State was sufficient.

Industry, agriculture, and commerce, along with a tourism campaign, were all reinitiated with an aggressive fervor. John desired for Newland to return to normal as quickly as possible.

The official drink of Newland, Crumley Cola, was provided gratuitously under government sponsorship in schools, restaurants, hotels, and wherever the beverage had previously been served. Newland had bought out the once Indianapolis-based bottler and now owned the brand.

Mary and the sons of the Sovereign were doing well despite some lingering concerns and fears from the ordeal they had recently experienced. The gripping fear, which embraced the first family of Newland, had taken a toll, but Mary resigned herself to the fact that she had accepted the risk when she agreed to marry John and, hence, wed Newland with him as well.

John prepared a speech to the nation two weeks after the apparent victory over the CBA. He wanted to be as sure as possible that no details had been overlooked in his thorough review of Newland's institutions, systems, and operations. He ordered Hinkins to attempt to locate Angel and invite her to the address and ceremony. Despite her desire not to receive public acclaim for her contribution, John deemed it appropriate to honor her. He privately rebuked his Sovereign Guard for not being able to locate her or the Private who had accompanied her. Hinkins, despite a thorough search, could not find a record of Angel in their citizenry logs or otherwise. The same proved true for the Private of his Guard. John was astonished that no one had asked for the full name of either person throughout their brief but crucial appearance during the CBA crisis. Hinkins promised to continue a vigorous search for both. John reminded him about his multiyear inquiry and pursuit of the CBA and his failures in that endeavor. Hinkins promised anew to locate the young lady who had been deemed the heroine of Newland.

John arrived with Mary and his two young sons at the Sovereignty Building for his address to Newland and the world. The entire Cabinet and legislature, as well as domestic and foreign dignitaries, were present.

With the world listening once again to this young nation, John addressed the thousands who awaited him in the front Square from the balcony of the Sovereignty Building. "For many in our nation and abroad, the past few weeks have been harrowing. I will be brief but succinct in my remarks. Our nation embarked on a magnificent quest, a journey from a country conceived from the onset on the basis of truth, justice, and principles of sound fiscal and moral leadership. Never in the course of human history has a brand-new nation experienced the growth, both materially and spiritually, that Newland has. Newland, as a nation, has allowed individuals with abundant talent to come here, grow, prosper, and contribute to the greatest experiment in the creation of the Ideal State. While I and, perhaps, others can envision such a state, to date, sadly, it exists nowhere. As we in Newland and, perhaps, other nations around the world so pursue such a goal, I do proclaim that we, in Newland, have made strides toward that perfection, which are evident in the lives of Newlanders, interactions with other nations, and all that is the totality of Newland.

"Recently, an unprovoked attack upon our nation threatened all that we are, as a people, as a nation, and as an ideal. I am thankful to report that the brutal and relentless war waged against us by a horrific foe is now over, and we have won. Not only have we prevailed against this unprecedented evil, but we also, as a nation, have emerged stronger, wiser, and even more committed to the maintenance of an ideal state. So many Newlanders gave their time, treasure, and talents to assist us in defeating this foe. Candidly, our friends and foes in the international community sat idly by as we teetered on the brink of extinction. Newland is mindful and cognizant of this sad reality and will weave the agnostic reaction of other nation-states into our future foreign policy. For now, Newland is secure, safe, and moving forward in the pursuit and attainment of the ideal state. We shall succeed in this mission and will leave an indelible mark on human history to prove that a nation reverent to God, committed to the best traits of mankind, and determined to use that state as a positive catalyst can and will triumph in the realm of human possibilities."

The crowd roared. John and Mary waved to their fellow countrymen with heartfelt, loving smiles. John was Sovereign. Newland, at present, was safe and prosperous, and the experiment of constructing, maintaining, and promoting a nation-state continued to flow like a current in a river bound for glory.

About the Author

Seven-term Congressman Chuck Fleischmann brings years of personal experiences from the practice of law, the world of politics, and interactions with world leaders to create stories filled with international intrigue and political drama. Fleischmann brings a unique perspective from his role as the Chairman of the Energy and Water Subcommittee of the Appropriations Committee. He has been married for thirty-seven years and has three sons.